Other books by Torrance Stephens

Novels & Novellas
a matter of attention
last from go

Short Stories
fast and gamin'
butter brown
rock star, stud, gigolo
freak type scene

Essays
dirt behind my ears
brilliant dumb
negro comfortable
nobel neocolonialism: u.s. west asian, north and east african
foreign policy under the obama administration
the legacy of the bush-obama keynesian dialect and income ine-
quality in america: a journal
The Rise of Establishment Politics: Essays On U.S. Politics During
the Bush and Obama Adminstrations

Poetry
for u who left me while I slept
late nite winds of club paradise
anonymous guest
FOr +h3 B1rds Poems in 140 ch4r4c+3rs Or l3ss: (For the Birds
Poems in 140 Characters of Less)

Plays
why I'm a ganster and other plays

History
The 3rd Republic: Nigeria's Transition to Democracy as Told By
National Print Media, 1992-1993

i

TORRANCE

A Matter
of Attention

STEPHENS

Acknowledgements: Andrea Hatter Cover

ISBN: PAPERBACK: 1-880861-01-1
THIRD PRINTING

RAW DOG BUFFALO PRESS
PALMETTO/MEMPHIS/WHEREVER
© 1987, 2000, 2016 BY
TORRANCE STEPHENS
@RAWDAWGBUFFALO

Love ya mom.

TTS

TABLE OF CONTENTS

QUOTE

"And yet so light steps across
The way her June feet pass
She does not bend the smoothest moss
Or bend the thinnest grass."

Countee Cullen

A Matter of Attention

By

TORRANCE STEPHENS

CHAPTER 1
DESOLATION

It was customary of me, in the squeamish, early mornings to find myself within the pecking range of my Apple. Normally, somewhere between eleven o'clock and one PM; slowly, but surely making a couple of few words and thoughts turn into a short story. Today an essay and tomorrow an epic, maybe even a perfidious mystery.

I don't know.

I don't know much of anything; about life or death, or sleeping and dancing. So why is it that I write? I have nothing to prove. I am already destined to fill the alarming void of an empty page. And it would be even more foolish to expect that this brilliant man of color, me, could ever receive fame and fortune via the sullen and interminable production of letters. It is what I prefer to do and I will continue to do so, in spite of the fact that I know that there exists an extant amount of editors out there that do not understand my experiences, and who have presupposed and decided that there is no reading public for me. This is about me, trying to stand on my box and dance on top of it.

The day was normal, nothing exceptional. The sun sang through the bellicose Oak leaves and the wind, platonically orchestrated, breezed through the poky city limits as if it were sand in a desert storm. I stepped into a pair of khaki slacks and extended my graceful appendages through the cable-knit charm of a flat grey cardigan sweater, completing the package with a pair of royal-blue high top Converse. And as if the sun itself, I found myself slipping through shadows, amid day dreams, within fantasies, atremble with rueful ambitions. Ambitions that even the great Poe could not produce from paper and pen. And before I lost their personality in the banality of a moments whisper, I lived them, and recorded them on disk.

1

I considered myself at all times to be genuine. However, I feel that authenticity was described best by Mr. Twain when he said: "I think we never become really and genuinely our entire selves until we are dead -- and not then until we have been dead years and years. People ought to start dead and then they will be honest so much earlier." I'm an honest being and I do not depend on anyone else -- except for a coupla' few million starving United States citizens. That's why I sell dope. Now don't be quick on the gun to judge my personal character and if you do, why don't you weigh it on the standard values of capitalism. This is a capitalistic country.

Firstly, I'm self-supporting and pay my taxes -- even if I don't agree with taxation without representation. Secondly, I realize that there exist, presently, a high rate of unemployment and hereby feel that giving my boys and younger mother fuckers the opportunity to make some money is extremely commendable on my part -- you don't need references to prove that you can work. Lastly, for more outrageous revelry, bud is probably the most practical buy on the market, inclusive of food, gas and other elicit contraband. I started off selling nicks and dimes but later moved up to the seven and twelve market. Reagan raised the prices and a lot of my dealer friend/associates blamed it on his reelection. Now its pounds and up. Well, I retract that statement. I would hook up one of my boys with something less than an elbow[1] - Fontain, Willie Mitch or Leon.

In general, I think that people in the U.S. are fucked up mentally, megalomaniacs and shit. They are quick to forget that back in the day -- 1839, to be exact, when Lin Tse-hsi ended that shit -- the U.S. made the Chinese by Opium. So what's wrong with a little blow and a little smoke? Nothing. But I can tell you one thing, as sure as my gas bill is high, that if the government legalized weed and blow that the deficit or what-

---

[1] Pound.

2

ever you call it, would eventually be el no longo. Already, the confiscated drugs in this country are second only to Exxon in total assets. The real deal is that Blacks make too much untaxable income. Politicians don't know what's up; that's one of the reasons I take my time to sit down and think, and write. Only because my sharp and exalted temporal facilities suggest that reflective remediation is deserved. Then I write, until the blackness of desolation exists no more. Maybe that is why I believe myself to be worthy of the title writer incessant, the story teller supreme. But then again G, maybe I'm just another "moderner," like the ones Jon Swift wrote about in reference to that famous *Battle of the Books*. A bowman, yea.

But any way, one thing about selling, I would always wake up and see the golden harvest of such a lucrative franchise. My car, my off-white 1971 Cutlass Supreme. Complete with spinners, tinted windows, alarm and an Alpine stereo system. It was the shit. The mother fuckin' shit. My car, my baby. If it had a pussy I wouldn't need the assistance of any of these rudy-poot, buck-teeth hoes. A babe ain't worth a shit no how. All they do is lie and bone. No good creatures, that's what they are, unless they are somebody's mother or grandmother. I would tell you about one but that would take us into the beginning of a new book. Butararr, you know, I got dressed and headed off to my boy Fontain's crib. Now Fontain is a mack, along with my boy Willie Mitch and myself, of course. They just' be tripping' all of the time, you know. They don't ever take nothing serious, you know what I mean?

Fontain was down, tight. He was the type of mother fucker who knew that Warren William was the original Perry Mason, and that the Greeks had no way of recording all of the philosophy that they stole. Thanks to Alexander the Great, no doubt.

He was my boy and he believed in me too. He read every piece I created and often compared me with Camus, Blassingame, and Dumas. Sometimes DuBois, when my creations would represent my most recent axiological contemplations. He lived in a plush crib down the street. So plush a crib that it made me sometimes wonder how I would be living if I would have completed medical school, and became a Psychiatrist. But I didn't and I was a drug dealer and a good one at that. After all, one don't break the law until they get caught. I guess writing and pushing dope are both kind of like death. "Les hommes sort tours condamne's a' mort avec des sursis indefinis".

Fontain was waiting outside in a fresh Converse warm-up suit, blue and white. He was putting some letters into his mail box.

"What you about?" I asked as I threw my car into park.

"Not a mus, not a mus. Just checking my mail box. Even a bat could see that. What's up with ya?" He rambled.

"Hurry up got damn it. You move like constipation."

"Constipate this mother fucker!" He exclaimed, holding his Johnston.[2]

"Fuck you. Don't get mad at me 'cause you slow as turtle fat!" I erupted wryly.

It seems like there is something about everything that I look at for longer than two seconds. That is what came to mind as I waited for Jones to finish what he was doing. I was ready to get to the Driftwood Inn and blend a little taste with the afternoon brunch crowd, know what I'm saying. I could always find someone, in particular a female of so compaction, to listen to the tales that I had awarded to print.

Just for a brief period, I looked at his door, just for a moment I mind you, and found myself aloft in the ruling arms of Vanity. She was talking to me, begging for me not to leave her. We were standing below the green lights of a street corner, and all that came to my

---

[2] Penis.

senses were the compromising sound of Shelia E's "*The Glamorous Life*".

She was occupied by a critically pink teddy and her legs stretched through the open atmosphere, touching the delicate liquid of my cornea. A mere scamper of flesh arched itself about in her scant covering of silk as the wind courted both nipples to attention. It was evident from the saliva, or whatever it was dripping from the side of her lips that we had just completed some act of selective sexual propagation, and that I had done an almost perfect detail.

"Why are you leaving?" She asked, patiently waiting for a reply.

"If you didn't want me to leave, you should have never entered the car, you were at your own risk. Besides, you can always go home and deal with your white concubine."

"Stay just a little bit longer." She stated, making each word smell of intercourse.

"I can't. I own a computer. Besides, being with one dame makes me feel as if I have been writing in the same color ink all of my life, or if I have only learned to master one type of software. Thanks, but no thanks."

"Man, you listening to this shit again?" Fontain asked as his slamming of the door took me away from my self-created pleasure.

"Man, let's listen to this." He continued. "Got the fresh tape. Shorty made it for me at the club the other night for three bills. Fire it up. I know that you got that truth, that killer, that Hinckley, the Wayne Williams."

"You know it! Tennessee flat-land, domesticated Sinsemilia. Can I ask you just one thing?"

"You already have but I will give you the benefit of the doubt. Continue." Fontain retorted.

"Do any of your clients over at the drug rehab suspect that you get popped?"

"I'm brilliant. Of course not. What is it, the salvation of man must be achieved on Earth, or something

5

like that? You ain't trying to play me fat are ya? Let me twist one up."

He proceeded to process the materials for consumption. I waited, looking at structures float by with the flickering of the dotted yellow lines. Every moment that I lived, experienced, made me seek refuge in paper and pen. Always it felt as if the most impersonal parts of my conscious appeared to come to mind when driving down the decomposed city avenues. On one side, there was the music pulsating from my six speakers, and on the other, narcissism, moderately blending with the thought of just knowing that motorist maneuvering by, could not penetrate the swarthy tint of my visual capsule.

The stiffly jointed beat took me back into the collective portion of my being. Taking me all the way back to the shores of the mother land -- Bilad as Sudan.[3] That was a hard beat, I tell you. A little Loose Ends mixed in with some NWA.

Both me and Fontain were in the mix, jerking our heads in opposite directions of our shoulders. Moving just enough to sedate our innate impulses. Then that smell came, the very exact smell that held me company on the so many days I received rejection letters. If I did not understand myself as well as I did, I would call a mother fucker like me crazy.

I'd say. "You dumb ass, stupid mother fucker. Why do you get the urge to write more when you constantly receive rejection slips? You ought to jus' stick to selling' dope!"

Yea, that's what I would say. But I don't and I do not have a reasonable response for the situation.

Anyway, the beat continued and Fontain had almost sucked down the entire joint.

"Hike!" I exclaimed in an attempt to initiate transference.

---

[3] Land of the Blacks.

6

"I did, and I called a bootleg. Be patient black. Jus' don't let the windows down and let the smoke out."

"You big chestier type mother fucker. You better pass me that."

"Here, take it, ya Jack Madden type mother fucker.

Like the smell of honey suckle in the late spring air, so was the flavor that entered the inner regions of my system. Sometimes I ridiculed Fontain about his profession. I like physicians too but I've always wanted to know what kind of people would visit, and pay a shrink with a name like Fontain? Real sick ones I figure.

But honestly, I guess that maybe I want respectability or stability. One of those social things that you only get through the precarious eyes of others. I could never quite comprehend this either. But I do know that whenever I think of psychology, I think of what my good friend Nietzsche saved for me.

> "What drives these psychologist forever in the same direction? A secret, malicious desire to belittle humanity, which they do not acknowledge even to themselves? A pessimistic distrust, the suspiciousness of the soured idealist? Some petty resentment of Christianity (and Plato) which does not rise above the threshold of consciousness? Or could it be a prurient taste for whatever is embarrassing, painfully paradoxical, dubious and absurd in existence? Or is it, perhaps, a kind of stew -- a little meanness, a little bitterness, a bit of anti-Christianity, a touch of prurience and desire for condiments?...But, again, people tell me that these men are simply dull old frogs who hop and creep in and around man as in their own element -- as though man were a bog. However, I am reluctant to listen to this, in fact I refuse to believe it; and if I may express a wish where I cannot express a conviction, I do wish wholeheartedly that things may be otherwise

with these men -- that these microscopic examiners of the soul may be really courageous, magnanimous, and proud animals, who know how to contain their emotions and have trained themselves to subordinate all wishful thinking to the truth -- any truth, even a homespun, severe, ugly, obnoxious, un-Christian, unmoral truth. For such truths do exist."

Every time I dwell on his remarks, I have to say thank you. I take it as a compliment and I am sure that Fontain and any of the boys would do the same. We try not to have or display emotions. But humor just seems to slip out of us, like passing' gas or something. It's not intentional but it is free entertainment. One could talk or write for years on the subject of comedy, cynicism, humor, or satire. See, what the average Jim Jones don't know is that not only can the average cat play basketball, but they are also probably a tad bit funnier than Eddie Murphy, or somebody famous like that. They just lack affiliations connected with issues of paternity.

"CLICK!!!"

The tape had abruptly ended, but I had auto reverse.

"Man!" Fontain remarked. "We would really want to check out this party tonight."

"What party?"

"This party that this babe that an associate of mine told me about. It's supposed to be live."

"Shit, that's our problem; we party to much and make our main objective issues of class and status. Anything to approximate Anglo-Saxons will do to us."

"Ain't you gone ask us where it is Dr. Harold Cruse Ben Jochannon?"

"Where?"

"1515 Mingo Place."

8

CHAPTER 2
DISTINCTION

"I am infinite. I am spaceless, I
am tireless; I am beyond body,
 thought, and utterance; beyond
all matter and mind. I am end-
less in bliss."
Paramahansa Yogananda

Fontain had taken the bawdy liberty, as he had with
me, to invite Black Magic and Willie Mitch to the party.
I was to meet them a little prior to eleven o'clock, at
black Magic's semi-Asian furnished flat.

They suggested that I wear something a tad-bit
more ornamental, and mere flashier than a warm-up
suit and Converse.

Until his first call, I was perched in front of my
desktop, reading a reasonable facsimile of a newspaper. I had become enthralled over some shit relating to
secular humanism and the P.T.L. Club. So taken over
by this article was I, that it prompted me to write an
essay of my own; regarding the purveyed stupidity one
would have to demonstrate to actually say, hypotheti-
cally, that "if my church don't get a gift' ten million dollars that the Lord will take me away because I failed
him." Strange to say the least, but even more strange is
the fact that someone with ten million bucks believed
the mother fucker. Anyway, I stored my tiny 750 word
essay on disk under the file "Oral", and broke.

Black Magic, commonly referred to by his associates in city hall as Mr. Monroe Boone, was standing
outside of his meager one car garage. Leaning on Fontain's metallic brown 911, flattening the captured tie
between the efficiently designed lapels of an Italian
suit. Its bluish, shark skin material, refracted the pinkness of the street light in such a manner that it seemed
to make his suit appear brown, off from a distance.

The swollen limpness of age-torn, Black Oak
branches, along with the opulence of a robust gather-

9

ing of nocturnal insects, fluttering around the contemptuous suspension offered by a fifty-watt light bulb, attracted my attention more so than the affirmed quart of brew that Willie Mitch coveted arrantly. The foible darkness, the cynosure of the shaded-suburban street and the random patterns of the insects, seemed to represent the wholeness of the universe that I had only observed in comic books and punctuation marks. "What are you bugging off of this time, ya string bean nose mother fucker?" It came from longtime associate William Mitchell. It was stated in a manner in which the wind directed it towards me

And I responded. Without the specious utterance of a single syllable, the slightest whisper. I firmly gripped my member with both hands. As if it were the last dollar on earth, and devoutly gripped my pipe and squeezed the sides of my crotch in a successful effort to provide three dimensional visibility. They laughed and the conversation went on from there.

Willie Mitch smiled and stretched his hands across the region of his belt with assured refinement. Glistening off the monumental gold rings on his hand was the rashness of the street light emissions. Finally returning his left foot to rest on the rubber floor board of his Cobra. His 289 Cobra. He was always talking shit about that car of his, as if he actually believed that a cat could be defined by the objects that they owned. Now it was sweet but it was not as suave bola as my Cutlass.

"My boy!" He shouted, extending his hand for a brief exchange of five. "You hurtin' them tonight."

"Sweet suit Black." Black Magic agreed, complementing his remark with an affirmative upward motion of his head. "What sustenance do you have on hold for the evening?" He asked.

My reason was still disposed to the previous accolades in reference to my attire. With my nakedness enthroned behind the arduous perplexity of a slightly over-sized, three-button, dry-gray seersucker suit, I reached my left hand in my upper-left inside pocket and in cant mode, tossed him nearly an eight-ball and two primos.

I did not really see what they saw in it. It really did not make a never mind on the money tip. I gave it to them all the time. To them, seven or eight years out of college was nothing more than another quick and gratuitous route to more avaricious theaters of action.

One was almost a district attorney, another, the accomplished physician and the last, my personal investment banker. And how did I manage to fit in, a penurious, self-proclaimed man of letters? I don't know. Pretending to be one thing, in fashion, habits and solitude, yet at the same time, making my living doing the equivalent of exchanging a NutraSweet package for C-notes.

"Man!" Fontain opened. "I have never been so insulted in my life, 'til today."

"What the fuck you crying about?" Monroe asked, questioning the infirmity of his character.

"I'm supposed to be professional jones around that hospital but yet they treat me like a client with no insurance. A Haitian client with no insurance."

"Bitch in charge made me take this personal inventory that just insulted my intelligence. She's just a counselor."

"Like commercials." I added.

He agreed, maintaining the same splash and peculation that he had started with to expound on his experience.

He continued. "Imaging, asking me if I feared confrontation, or if I made silly mistakes, or if I ever feel the inability to express myself. Express my dick test maker!!!" He ended, holding the region of his jewels.

"Man, fuck that shit. You still a mack. We know it and the world knows it. That's why they always trying to make it hard, and painful for us." William commented, expanding on his views with the aid of some Pope that I suspect he accidently learned.

"Weak foolish man! Will
Heaven reward us there
With the same trash mad
Mortals wish for here."

"Didn't know that they wrote shit like that in the Wall Street Journal." I remarked, accepting silently, Monroe's approval of the powder. "Tell me this, did Fontain tell you who was throwing this party? It better be swinging 'cause I could have just cooled out at the crib with Tiana and the Cary Grant film festival."

"Shit, you already got all of his movies on tape. You shouldn't be tripping." Fontain stated in an intruding tone. "That shit happened back in the day when T.V. went off before dinner. That shit don't go off no more."

I played him fat until an appropriate response to my question was uttered from his lips.

"One of the board members, the only one of dark complexion, if you know what I mean ...He's celebrating his sister's birthday." Fontain completed, accepting the package from Black Magic.

"What's his name?" I questioned, hanging my head to the beat of some tune to which its name I did not know.

"Does it matter? Names aren't worth a shit until Webster or New Heritage get a hold to them." Monroe carefully, fervidly explained. Also moving his head to the same pulse bellowing from the auto.

We all remained there, not talking about much, reanimating every note, every beat, comprehending the total prism of each other's movement. They were not interested in riding with me, in my Cutlass to the party. Regardless of its capacity to entertain selectively, six persons in anomalous comfort, they preferenced that we ride in twosomes.

Fontain, and even Willie Mitch, on isolated junctures, had taken me to the local Porsche dealer, in hopes of me purchasing what they assigned as a "real car". Willie even made a comparison between my Apple and the admired vehicle, advocating that with such a machine, I could create and participate in intimate experiments of friction and velocity. So sold on the car was he that he actually perceived that it was the final manifestation of the rib "Jones" used to make humans six thousand sum odd years ago. He did not know that other ribs existed, years before the human order that he spoke of, that were manufactured in Asia and Africa.

"Move that shit to the side mother fucker." Willie stated.

"Suck the side of my dick you no license having bitch." He laughed.

Laughing was the shit. I think that it was what we did better than anything, and I mean anything. Boning, eating, and sleeping. Anything was subject to splendiferous ridicule and absurd speculation. Anything! Death, politics, and religion more so than all the other bull shit that we encountered. Like that shit Fontain was just dwelling upon. A mother fucker don't even begin to understand how offending it is to a nigger, to be asked "if he feared confrontation." Shit, we live on confrontation. As a matter of order, it is such an ordained portion of our psyche, our anima that it has for us, important nutritional value.

It fills one's veins, similar to the supernatural way fields of Blue bonnets stray along the middle and sides of highways, in unbridled parts of Texas. It places one eye to eye, side by side, and fist to fist with reality. Just ask any mother fucker who tried to get in the Air force Academy, prior to 1981 that had the Sickle-Cell trait. They'll tell you about confrontation and reality and humor and self. See, in real life activity, there exist no laws of engagement. Whatever the mind can perambulate is permitted.

Sometimes, when the law get too close, or when a babe tries to make me into the opposite of what I am - - "wrong of wrongs", I confuse reality with dreaming. I even think that I know what Shapiro's *Bourgeois Poet* pontificated when he stated:

"THE ONE WHO HAS DREAMED ME HAS NOT
PUT ME BACK."

But one thing for sure, at least for the time being, I know for a fact that "jones" had nothing to do
with it.

Some of the shit that we had discussed and
some of the stuff that I had been thinking about was
worth me writing down on paper.

I had managed to slip a small note pad out of
my outer pocket.
I started to scribble when suddenly, Monroe yelled.

"What you writing down now?"

He approached me, trying to read what I was
writing. I hated for people to look over my shoulder
and read what I was writing. It made me want to stab
the eyes out of the culprit with an ink pen. They always wanted to read the shit that I thought, at the
moment of its creation. Never when the idea was polished and exhibited through short stories and poems
printed out via a thermal transfer printer.

"I'm writing about the moon and of this party
that we are supposed to be blending too." I retorted in
an unctuous voice.

"The next Spike Lee!" Fontain threw out abruptly.

"Man, fuck you and Spike Lee. Don't be trying
to compare me to nobody else."

"Aw mother fucker, wasn't nobody thing to dog
you. Take it as a compliment." Fontain replied.

"Fuck that shit, that man ain't even a real writer.
He's just another funny mother fucker from New York
that got the access to make films. All the reviews I've
read, about his flicks, have been on the "Up-n-up"
though. We're different, I'm up there with Voltaire and
Tolson and he's not."

The music, still priggishly commanding the in-
different motion of our structures, yielded the inspiration inside of Monroe to meet Willie Mitch half way in
front of the car, to repeat the seemingly perpetual,
round of bumps. In the process, he struck an admira-

tion for the dark black sun glasses supported on Willies bucket sized head. He put them on his face and weighed their appearance militantly.

"These are some heavy glasses." He remarked, with hands gently dropping from the sides of the frames.

"That's because they are the real deal." Willie retorted with stern confidence.

"Oh, so they are original heavy glasses made and manufactured by the real iron workers." He replied with a laugh.

"You stupid mother fucker, real Ray Bans."

He then turned to me and asked. "B. L., do they look good on me; do they match my suit?"

"Man, nothing looks good on you. Face it."

Trying to put a little more seriousness in the conversation, in an attempt to shutter the laughing, he continued.

"So you think it's my head? My head don't look right in these glasses? It can't be my suit; I am as clean as a board of health."

"Yes nigger, it's yo' head. Your head looks like this."

Fontain accented his statement by holding up a closed fist and ended. "You got a fist head mother fucker!!!"

"It's almost 12:30. We better get going." Willie suggested.

I followed. "Let's stop and get some brew on the way. I'm not driving."

"Yea, you ride with me", Willie said, starting the engine of his deadly reptile.

"Stop somewhere we can get it cheap." Fontain ordered, now, turning the key to his ignition.

"Yea!" I exclaimed, from the passenger side. "Ya'll follow us to the store then ya'll take attack formation from there." I continued, now completely out of the drive, car aside car.

"Whatever's cheap." he repeated.

15

"We're at the crib, let's spare no expense, we're getting Stag." I ended.

Zooming down the street, with the air crushing through the open windows and into my face, a renewed excitement for the evening again prevailed. The risqué textures of the shrubs and trees flashed by like slow movements in the presence of a strobe. And the lights blurred from intersection to intersection, as if exposed to some time-lapsed purl. And once more, the music, loud, eccentric and forfending, sat with me, around my body tighter and more secure than the seat belt straddled around my waist. This time it was Grace Jones and "*Slave To The Rhythm*."

It made me think about the video and the creativeness that it expressed. The next thing I know, the music is blending out, and I'm actually placing myself in inventive dialogue with Spike Lee, in his New York apartment discussing our joint effort on a movie that I had written. He was arched at the end of a light-maple, rectangular table, which appeared to serve as desk and bar. He rubbed the bottom of his chin in a manner that would require several views from under a microscope if detailed discernment was required and sipped loudly from an icy Heineken bottle.

Sounding like a native Queen's rice crispy, he looked boldly through those thuggish spectacles of his, flared his nares several times, and said. "B. L., looks like we got a winner in this."

"I know what you mean Spikie baby. But I just don't understand the logic behind making a three-D movie in black and white."

"B. L., B. L., don't worry, I won't dis' ya. I went to film school didn't I? What's the trip anyway, C. B. S.[4] the only ones gettin' taxed up in this mother fucker."

Me and Spike were laughing together. Bull shitting and getting paid for it. Just like Dave Letterman.

---

[4] Caucasian Broadcasting Service

"Since I get the most ink in the headlines", he said, "It is only fair that I get 70/ 30 on the film and 50/ 50 on publication rights."

"You talk like a fish", I irked in a high pitch tone. "If anything, I get 80% of all publication royalties and rights, and 60% of the film. I'm a writer, what's up with that?"

The roads moderately begin to penetrate my visual path. We turned into the filling' station across from Starvin Marvin and eventually made our way to the party.

CHAPTER 3
DIVINITY

We approached the foundation of the cottage innocently, invading the wall-like confinement of giant
twin azaleas, conquering a small stream of water that
had resulted from the late night use of strategically
placed, mushroomed shaped garden sprinklers. As if
Amenhotep III[5], Fontain, b/ k/ a[6] cookie head, guided
our path through the indelible rock gardens and small
patches of cultivated wild flowers. Monroe was rapidly catching up with him while Willie and me straggled
not too far behind.

The house, with its classic Victorian grace, partly
enclosed by a carapace of glass, had extended from its
side, a huge awning. We walked pass its poles and
held pose. On my right, were twenty or more circular
cafe tables. Each companion to an off-white table cloth,
candle, and coffee settings for two. Pairs of wire-
framed lawn chairs, also vividly white in hue, flanked
each table as if in parade formation.

Desperate people and events were scattered
about randomly, with most individuals migrating and
cooling' out in the region to my extended left, adjacent
to one of the wet bars.

"Not bad, ay?" Fontain sighed.

"Bros need a rubber neck 'round this mother
fucker." Monroe complemented.

"We have ignition." I completed.

"I don't think that I have enough energy for all
of this." Willie stated. "Where's that package?"

"Settle down", I said. "If you need energy,...That's why you hold yo' dick, 'cause your dick
give you energy that you never knew you had. Ay?"

---

[5] (1417 - 1379 BCE)Husband of Queen Tiye of 18th Dynasty of
Egypt
[6] Better Known As.

19

"Man, I'm gonna get a drink." Fontain remarked. "I'm gonna go and mingle with one of these freaky things and be on my way."

Monroe unerringly, agreed. "I'm with ya. I got your back home boy, don't even trip."

I had not been in the insensate[7] company of so many delicious looking black women since the Hearns/ Hagler fight. Women, on most opportunities, seemed to bring out the premium side of my devotion. Yet this time, there were so many, and they were so plentiful , in every style, make and model imaginable. In multitudes, they flourished around the patio area, flaunting the best of Chanel, Perry Ellis, Patrick Kelly, and other internationally acclaimed fashion designers. And all it seemed, had pocketbooks with initials that did not correspond to their names.

One was in blue, persisting rejuvenated next to a fountain, falling, and grinning squeamishly to the custodial flattery proffered by two gentlemen. The yellow outdoor lights of the fountain glistened off of her presumable varnished, soft-cotton tunic and from her established cymbal-like earrings, as she sternly swung her head in an attempt to shift the hair from in front of her eyes. Buttons climbed up the base of her skirt as if an ordered column of larger than usual golf tee's were implanted along the dorsal segment of her lower half. Her impeccable hips offered to the skirt a sense of efficiency that even starch could not attain.

Willie Mitch had discovered a yellow rose and was doing everything in his prowess to sale his product to her. With her hair pulled back, braided and wrapped in gold silk, analogous to the way horses legs were taped on race day, she praised his conversation with the reticent attention of both eyes, with her lips parted expectantly. I had overheard someone say that Stevie Wonder was present and as a gift, would perform a special song in honor of the birthday girl. Under the green and white stripped awning, I observed a

---

[7] Senseless. Unconscious.

crowd of people hoarded around this man with dark glasses and long, reputed braids. Instantly, I concluded that this sugar attracting the ants was Mr. Wonder. It was sort of a trip and all, bros and sisters just standing around and gaiting at Stevie as if he was some [8]avatar. And what was more enjoyable, astonishing and amazing to me was the fact that he could not see them.

After all of the practical angles of my present position were reviewed and doubled-checked for accuracy, I walked scantly to where Fontain and Monroe were standing. Both appeared to be momentously rooted into the earth. Monroe with cigarette in hand and Fontain, embellished with the ostentatiousness furnished by a vodka martini. They too were busy scoring the success of Willie's efforts.

"Beep, beep, beep, beep, beep, beep, beep."

"Man, cut that shit off." I said in reference to Fontain's beeper. "You should invest in one that vibrates."

"You forget that I am in a respectable trade. If I get stopped by the law, I can just tell them that I am a physician and it won't be no trip."

"All of these hoes around here and ya'll dumb ass mother fuckers talking about beepers. I question severely sometimes, why I swing with ya'll." Monroe said in a cursory voice.

Pointing up at the bosom of stairs beyond the primary group of sliding terrace doors, Fontain remarked. "See jones up there, standing with the babe and that guy with the white people hair? That's him , the one throwing this bash. The babe standing next to him is his sister. She's the birthday slim."

He was an over-sized gentleman. He was panoplied in a royal blue wool blazer, grey pleated slacks and a pink, bold stripped button-downed oxford. While looking at him, I could not help to make the bland comparison between he and Tubby Bowling, the character in George Orwell's *"Coming Up For Air"*. If

---

[8] Hindu. God/ Goddess coming to Earth in some bodily form

George was there with me, he would have described him, as he did Tubby Bowling, as "a fat man who is thin on the inside." I was not one for stereotyping but from the way in which Fontain had described him, I could feel that his personal character was suspect.

Tubby's boy was lined along his right, also outlined in a royal blue blazer. A lenient black turtle neck appeared to control his intercurrent motion along with the systematic exactness of his cuffed khakis. The woman, holding herself in such a stance to renounce the both of them, eminently scanned the spicy flock of restrained members of the local bourgeois. She did not notice me. It might have been the dredlocks.

"She's finer than amug?" I commented, now giving my attention to the owner of an abrasive brown, button front cotton-knit dress. Making me want to transcribe myself into Spiderman; so that I could better stick to the inside of her sentient being--as did the material fibers of her outfit.

Monroe finished his square and buried it in the Bermuda grass with one of his Cole-hans. With a funnel of smoke racing from his lungs he remarked, "I just want to lick her all over for a whole week and I'll be cool."

"Don't make me earl. If pussy was meant to be eaten, a mother fucker could pick it up from the deli section of Kroger." I noted. "What's her name Fontain? She's finer than a mother fucker."

"I think it is Margarita. Margarita Fine." He retorted.

"You've got to be joking." I answered.

"But don't get your dick on hard. I think that she is blending with jones in the turtleneck. Besides, you got to spend big paper if you want to get slim. She's the kind of Dame that a nigger got to spend three grand on just to find out the color of her panties."

"Fuck that shit." I continued. " If I got to spend three K on her then, the bitch better put some aluminum siding on my crib."

"You be tripping too hard!" Monroe exclaimed. "Let's go get Willie and go inside for a little while. Everybody keep looking at us when we laugh."

"That's 'cause you laugh like a seal." Fontain pointed out.

"Fuck you", he returned. "I'm not going to take that kind of shit from a nigger with lips the size of an album cover. All you need is auto-reverse and I could play a tape in 'em."

Inside, I saw her for a second time, positioned next to a giant glass cable atop the polished stairs. She looked nice, real nice. Prancing down that spiral stair well, and about the area as if she was the first draft of an abstract piece of art. Not knowing herself, what she meant, not knowing what she was about, or any of that kind of shit.

Looking at her from the ground level was like waiting for the phone to ring. Abound with an ample supply of detail and lewdness, her stalwart partiality depicted itself to be worth more than the three thousand dollars spoken of earlier. The hemline of her mini-skirt circled her thighs as if it had been drawn with a compass. Coupled with a pair of clogs and a sleeveless blouse, she most certainly isolated her sinuous[9] yet smartened; tender yet epicurean difference from the bevy of babes she encountered at the foot of the stairs.

I wanted her so bad that she entered for a brief moment, into the confined ranges of my subconscious. I do not know what actually was going on with my being. Sometimes I even thought that my terse passage into the subliminal depths of my existence were so real, that they could even be recorded on Polaroid film. If such were the case, my life style would benefit Spiderman when he said:

> "...Nowadays I cruise around
> for some action to get into, so I

---

[9] Curvy.

can photograph myself in that action....So I can sell those photos to the Daily Bugle, so I can pay my rent...which is always."

My rent is never late.

The more that I looked into the discreet aura of her structure, the more my day dream penetrated my view.

We were slanted against a small cluster of rocks, with the sand flowing between our toes with each passing of the waves. In an area with plenty of passionate coastline, an island perhaps. Caracas. Lamu. Corpus Christi. The Blue-Stone counterfeit equivalent of a bathing suit attempted in vain to protect her lasciviousness.

Caressing the inside of her dampness with my toes, she freely placed her flesh against mine and spoke to the sun in a foreign tongue. Alternating her ritualistic sounds with the motion of her permed, wet, and salty hair, illicitly aside the eviction of my face.

And there was music. Yes. Sade. "*Cherry Pie*"--I believe it is called, was bouncing through the breeze like pelicans gliding from palm to palm.

By the time the music of the band had awakened me, she was gone. Moroe came up to me and remarked.

"Fontain told me to get you and take you up stairs."

"What's upstairs? Where is Willie?"

"He's still out back blending with that babe."

I followed him up the stairs, past a small collection of Morris Louis' reproductions. Each stripe and blotch and color and pattern seemed only to remind me of slim in the mini skirt. Her legs gave man a visual buzz. Her eyes carried with them a variation of agile dispositions.

Additional sketches lined the hallway, but this time I could not discern their apprentices. Lacking in color, the polarizing effect they stirred in me seemed to be more powerful, more portly than the hue filled collection bordering the steps. I heard laughter emanating through the door approaching our immediate left. Monroe entered.

The platonic aroma of that vegetable of knowledge filled my senses, as did the pleasurable view of five or more captivating creatures of remorse and tumid personalities. The one called Margarita Fine was standing in front of a full-length mirror, alluringly brushing her hair with several fingers, checking for panty lines and the sort. Fontain approached her and whispered into her ear. She turned around, smiled and looked at me as if I was about to spend money on her. A lot of money. She walked into the bathroom with two of her girls. Fontain followed signaling for us to join them. I did not see either of the two gentleman that had flanked her earlier.

It was a large rest area, with a fifty gallon aquarium built in the wall above a brown marble, sunken bath. Pink and green towels, adorned with grey and green flowers, lined the bottoms of every mirror, every basin.

Fontain led with formal introductions. They wanted to purchase an eight ball. That is when I first heard her speak.

"That is a very nice suit." She commented in a raucous, Americanized, French accent.

I guess that she thought that such a remark would get her a better buy. It did. I gave it to them for two bills. She smiled and the others returned to the private recesses of the bedroom. We were alone.

She watched perniciously form her toilet seat as I counted the money. Her legs raised and crossed like an infant, and her eyes followed her hands as they stroked the lower portion of her calves.

"What is your name? Do you know James or Robert?" She asked as the rubbing of her thighs stopped.

Stiffly I returned. "Gash Love and no."

A peculiar locution bloomed in her smile. "Your name rings of romance Mr. Love."

"I might be a romanticist, or nematocyst[10], what ever comes first. But as for love, in tennis, love is equivalent to zero. Nothing."

"You speak in riddles but you know of love. I can see it in your eyes. And can smell it in your cologne."

"I won't believe that until Santa Claus and Jesus Christ tells me. It was nice meeting you Miss Fine."

I looked around to make certain that I did not leave anything and headed for the door.

"Wait a moment." She opined, removing herself from her perched position. "Where are you going?"

"Home."

"How can I get in contact with you. Just in case I need your professional services."

I pulled out of my pocket, my faithful note pad and tore off a half a sheet. I scribbled my telephone numbers down and handed it to her."

"The first one is my beeper number. The second is at home. Do you know how to work a beeper number?"

She jiggled her head in confusion.

"Just call me at home and I will explain it to you in detail. My ride is probably looking for me."

"I bet she's worried."

"Yea, I'll bet he is."

"Well again, it was a pleasure."

"Mr. Love..."

"Yes."

"Do you know where the Blue Bar is located?"

"Yes, over on the 3100 block of New York Avenue."

"Maybe we can meet there, tomorrow for lunch. To teach me more about the beeper, oui? That is, if you would like to join me"

"Why, are you coming apart?"

---

[10] Stinging cell of the Hydra.

CHAPTER 4
PROMINENCE

She said that she wanted to meet me in an indiscreet location. Near the spitting control of the lake front and away from the ruling animation of the local university. The Blue Bar, and its overbearing animation, was neither of the two. It was powerful and held within its atmosphere, a nostalgic terror.

The sun seemed to be a part of the boyish determination that I had designated to direct my physical scowl. It was only ten minutes away yet I had never entered its doors. It was like being in show business for twenty nine years and not recalling how to write a single musical note. Must be something in the air that makes me want to change my mind about things I perceived to be once true. Like the simple way I felt when I had coasted all of my life that I would never go out on a date.

By dubious[11] means, I had just acquired the permanent use of a 66 T-Bird that had been donated to me, so kindly by a post-humous client. Even Monroe and Fontain gave it their blessings. Polished black with broad white walls. Its beige interior was fitting enough to accommodate me, three of my boys and a case of quarts actively.

I had missed the ESPN sports update and felt it only acceptable that I stop by a convenient store and pick up a quart of Stag. One can always locate Stag easily, by walking all the way down to the end of the beer case. There it would be resting, in frigid peace, next to all of the other quarts going for 99 cents or less.

My next stop would be the post office. I had rented a P.O. box to insure that my literary correspondence would be flexible enough to meet my de-

---

[11] Suspicious.

mand for rejection letters. Don't get me wrong, I trusted the postal service. So much that on numerous occasions I had mailed special friends half pound samples of goods through the center of cut out cook books, and I must admit that the services were very efficient, and inexpensive.

With the company of an icy cold quart of brew in my lap, my mail and an ink pen behind my ear, I headed for the lake front. It seems as if massive bodies of water filled my lungs with a richness that even Huges or Chekhov could not describe. It was as if I could smell sounds, smokey mosaic sounds that only the fasting man can adequately taste; penetrating the palate with an ironic effect that can be read in every neurotic ripple, every lonesome wave.

Expecting the best, I opened the envelope with the bright orange M.C.I. pasted in the upper left-hand corner. The others were rejection letters, three rejection notices. So far, that is six for the week, seven for the month and twenty-five for the year. The last one was from this local fiction contest. Its purpose was to inform me that I had been rewarded the second place prize of $100. it was not the first time that I had won or placed in a writing complexion. It was wickedly bazaar however, that I had been recognized in complexion but not by editors.

"Any writer," so said James Baldwin, "I suppose feels that the world into which he was born is nothing less than a conspiracy against the cultivation of his talent....On the other hand, it is only because the world looks on his talent with such a frightening indifference that the artist is compelled to make his talent important."

I think that I understand what he is saying, but as for the world, I could give a flying hopper grass fuck. I know that I can write, that I can tell a story, and that I am the only one who can tell it the way that I can, but what about the blind man who cannot see the dance.? Or the person who perceives the church as a building and not the people? Is there a universal, an axiological[12] law that states that others determine what you mean, discern what you are actually stating? Maybe someone on Pennsylvania Avenue does not like me. And since they don't they can suck on "these"[13] until I get some answers.

1:05 PM. I walked in the restaurant. The timid and magnetic template of cooling brown cedar and the fragrance of perfumes and tobacco, did very little to improve my mood. Ambling past a platoon of pay phones and the bar, I contrived to rèsumè my vested demeanor. I did not notice her at first.

Suspended in the unsullied noon light, she was seated at a table fixed for two, with the gentleman Fontain had identified as her brother. They were beside the wall, prior to the patio section. Above them, strongly abetted by a steel blue acrylic frame, was a billing for an expired jazz festival and a rectangular sun pore.

Her slim, coke-bottle shaped figure, the vainglorious cut of her calm, black hair and her expressive, fertile body movements, attracted my reserved nature like iron fillings to a magnet.

A red, semi-pleeted, calf-length skirt, with huge extended pockets--at least on the left side, and a silky brown, crewneck, silk shirt pronounced the caramel dignity of her skin. By the time she noticed me, I was almost near the setting. Her hand was extended waving and banging together severely, several obtuse wooden bracelets.

I though that you had forgotten," she said. Standing up with her brother to introduce us.

"Jimmi, this is Mr. Gash Love. He came to the party with Fontain." She continued, holding on to my arm with both hands as if she had known me half of her life.

---

[12] Study of the nature of value judgements.
[13] Reference to scrotum sac.

Extending his hand he revealed. "Yes, Fontain and I work together. Yes, a very fine Physician. But his golf game is fucked."

"Jimmi, that sounds horrible." She blustered like a loving sister.

He hunched his shoulders and continues. "He tells me that your game is fairly respectable."

"Fairly," I retorted, nodding my head in agreement.

He was of medium height and carried with him, I'd say, about sixty pounds more than he needed. His appearance, however was not potent enough to counteract the crowded enchantment Margarita's voice spurred inside of me. I looked at her hands, and then into her sturdy dark black eyes.

James asked, "So what type of work are you in? Fontain tells me that you are quite a writer."

"I peck here and there."

"Is that how you support yourself?"

"No. I was left a small dowry by my grandparents and make profits, enough to live on, through commodities."

Margarita giggled with contempt, tightening her grip on my hand.

"Smart move. Take care of your investments. I must be going. Another board meeting you know. Besides, I think this seat is for you."

He departed. We sat down.

"Commodities?" She questioned.

"Yes. Goods from the land, you know."

"I didn't know that you were a writer. I never placed you any where in front of your beeper." She stated, playing with the string of pearls around her neck.

I wondered what was it about me that made me welcome to spend a day in the life of her alter-ego.

"I forgot my beeper so we will have to do something else. Let's order, I'm starved."

"We have all of the afternoon together."

"That's what you think."

"What do you write about?"

"Everything. The sun, trees, the moon,....just thinking. I write about myself. Writing is reflective. It takes away my problems inside my head and places them on paper, and keeps them there for me to laugh at, for future reference."

"Do you ever find the spirit to write about women?"

"Sometimes. Mostly gangsters though."

"So tell me something now, how are the hotels in Paris? They sure look great on postcards. I had the chance to go there once."

"Les hotels sont bons a Paris." The way she talked made my pants swell. But I managed to play it off.

"I'm sorry," she remarked. "Do you speak any French?"

"I know of only one phrase other than oui, ...Une Francaise."

She blushed and eventually ordered a light salad and tea. I requested fried clams and Crown Royal on the rocks.

Mostly huddled with white people, the environment made me wonder for a moment. All of my life, I had lived with white people, eaten with them in the same restaurant and yet we lived our lives as if two poles on the same magnet. The conversation furthered.

"I've only been in America for three years now. I was born in Brazil and went to school in France. Mummy would not have it any other way."

"So I guess that explains your sumptuous dialect."

"Dialect?"

"Yes, the way you speak?"

"So, that's why you paid little attention to me at the party. You were listening to me. You're the first man to ever listen to me. At work, they crowd me into a stubborn and rigid little closet. They call it an office. And my brother, just like our father, wants to be protective. So he thought, when he made the decision to send me to Paris for law school."

"Where did you learn to speak English?"

"In France."

"Sounds likely."

She drew her hand from her neck and placed it flatly on the table and remarked. "Don't compare me to no one else." From the pitch of her voice, one could easily discern that she did not accept my casual remark pleasantly."

She continued. "I'm not like those..."

"Ah ha, those. So you represent the those of them."

"Them?"

"Yea, them. Like the giant ants."

"Ants?"

"Yea, ant. The movie."

"I never got out to see it."

"I'm sure, it came out about in the fifties."

"What was it about?"

"About these giant black ants in the desert raping and pillaging. It was an alright flick."

"You don't strike me as the type."

"What type?"

"The Viking type. Raping and the sort."

"How do you know? I could imagine you, say for instance, in a day dream. A day dream recorded on disk, in the form of a short story, where all names and places are of a fictitious sort. There I could create rape. Rape so vivid that when you would read it, it would make you drip, and sweat all over. It is possible."

"Do you ever look at Dr. Ruth?" she asked with her head tilted a little bit to the left.

"No." I returned quickly.

"Well", she said. "You do know of her, oui?"

"We."

"If you had one question to ask her, just one question in the entire world, what would you ask her?"

Without any hesitation what so ever, I retorted. "First, I'd get within a whisper of her ear and ask, 'Dr. Ruth, sugar,...what's your favorite position?'"

Her eyes carried, if anything, a faint breeze. her smile, a cant indication of a sparkling mind. As a writer, in particular a male writer who explores the depths of adventure to the extent of subliminal lasciviousness[14], as I select to consider myself; the first priority to consider is the female encounter. Frankly, if it were not for them, I doubt if I could tender the urge to record my perspectives in words.

Some check my spelling, others act as critics, still more enjoy the materials. It would be reasonable to assume that the reason that I have very few hard copies around, other than copyrights, is because people-- mostly women and my boys--keep them.

Getting back to our conversation, Margarita was explaining to me the ins and abouts of her favorite soap opera. I had learned that she was a lawyer and that she and her brother shared the house. And that the other gentlemen craved her structure so much that he gave her a pear-shaped diamond. She had been stringently affected by material contamination.

"So what's the use of playing them every day? It's not like the play offs or nothing important." I returned, commenting on her rational in support of daytime soaps.

Softly, "see, it has to be like that so the girl can get the guy in the end."

"Oh, I get it. Mack scene, mack scene, mack scene."

"Um hum! Until she gets the guy."

"So, I take it that that is when the trouble starts."

She laughed as she rubbed her metallic rust polished fingernails against one another.

"What do you look at?" She questioned.

---

[14] Of or characterized by lust.

33

"Not too much. I have a computer. Its just like a T.V. except that I can correct anything I think to be an error."

"You have to prefer something. Tell, me, what is it?"

"Well, Nova, or anything on P.B.S., BET or ESPN. Sports, Jerry Lewis and Dean Martin Movies. Black classics."

"See I told you." She remarked as if she had won some type of holy war. "What else?"

"Frankenstein Jr. It's pretty cool having an "anti-ray" for every ray sent at you. Dr. Who. . ."

"Dr. Who?"

"Yea, Dr. Who. You've never checked out Dr. Who?"

"No, it's probably on when my stories are on?"

"No baby, it's a lot deeper than that. It comes on at about eleven."

"What's it about?"

"Baby, need I not remind you that Dr. Who is a space traveler caught up in a space/ time continua." I drew my arms around me in a manner that would have resembled Zoro holding his cape in front of his face, just for a little excitement.

I did not know what to expect from her. At the time, it seemed as if slowly but definitely, the world was regressing back to a state similar to the dark ages. Especially since more than fifty percent of all citizens believed that scientist were dangerous because they knew too much. Only the clouds knew what they thought of writers. Rain forbid.

Margarita was getting impatient.

"I'd wish that he'd bring something to snack on before I start nibbling on you. And you ain't nothing but bones." She commented in a joking manner.

"Humph, I might be skinny but the meat that I have is prime. It'll be a good meal, I tell you that, and full of protein."

The waiter brought the food.

"Are clams like oysters?" She asked curiously fascinated with the dishes.

"Some what. Both are from the phylum Molluska."

"I can't eat raw oysters, can you?"

"I figure that if I can kiss a babe, I can eat raw oysters."

"That's not the same."

"Yes it is. What's up with your gentleman friend. Not like I'm concerned but the glare of that diamond is about to blind me. I see it, just cool out on the flashing shit. He's got to have plenty of paper. What does he do?

"He's not your competition. He works with the Department of Justice."

Instead of going on with the discussion, I paused and let my mind run astray. I was familiar with infamous dice agents through mystery stories and High Times Magazine. This department of the government had successfully replaced the constitutional right to bail with preventive detention, and by-passed the courts in allowing drug seizures up to 100 grand. They had throughout history, avoided commissions like the Indian Hemp Commission of 1894 and the LaGardia commission of 1968. Their actions, in my mind, were synonymous to the way kudzu grows in the south.

"He's not my match but he likes me." She replied, rolling the stone portion of the ring in, with her thumb, closer to her palm. I suspect that she thought that I would forget about it all together. She probably did not know that I could give a flying grass hopper if she was engaged or not. But that's our secret. O.K..

"I bet he's a bama.[15]"

"What's a bama?" She questioned sincerely.

"You know, the kind of guy that has a good job, money, false friends, twenty credit cards and who would buy a woman anything she wants. Especially if

---

[15] Homely and soft Mother fucker.

she appears to be worthy of ones visual and physical dedication."

"No, he's a real nice person."

"Yea, that's what I said."

"Comtez-vous rester ici longtemps?" I take it, she was asking a question. Startled mostly and still hungry, I returned "Huh? Are you referring to go?"

I offered to pay for the meal but she suggested otherwise. Avarice followed her every motion, seduction her virtuous gift. She asked for my number again and signed it in her address book. I liked her, she was hard. She carried a black book too.

Margarita had all of the attributes of a full-developed beauty. Wide, spontaneous lips. a flatly-round nose and a pair of wary dimples, that collapsed when ever her mouth would open. Her mannerisms were those of the most refined woman. The operative world, in conjunction with her self-esteem, and the discomfort that they sparked, represented the realistic and interminable forces heir to her personal visions.

We drove around the flashy city streets, past package store after package store after package store. Margarita had established herself as being tasteful and played convenient attention to my statements. She only wanted to know about drugs and writing.

"Do you get high? I didn't see you,. . . at the party."

"Every now and then, but only bud. It's my livelihood, I can't afford to. Beside, people buy it like that." I snapped my fingers. "I'm small time. A can move a few pounds of smoke or a few grams of blow."

She turned inward, towards me. I told her of my daydream.

"When I first saw you, I could not penetrate your structure, so I dreamed of you and I."

Fascinated, she commented. "No, no, I saw you in the yard, next to the insect killer. You were paying specific attention to quite a few of the guest. Or looking at the ultra-violet light when it fired a poor bug to death."

36

"No seriously, it was you and I. In the Congo or on Lamu."

"Lamu?"

"A beautiful little Arab colony off of the coast of Kenya. A writer's paradise."

"So tell me, was I watching you write?"

"For a little while, but you took all my ink."

She wanted to drive around forever, asking me questions as if she was reporter for the Amsterdam News. She was quick to insert little legal jokes concerning my method of free-enterprise. It was embarrassing to consider that her face had completed the rites and rituals of professional school.

Margarita suggested that we stop at this abandoned gas station, on the south shore of the lake.

Such sun splitting imagery was made to be photographed; Margarita and the Thunderbird, encapsulated in the verdant conformity of the wilderness. Even the wild, and the outdoors, by themselves, in either night or day, was just as paramount.

I leaned aside the car and prepared to smoke a splif. We passed it between us, five times, before it was gone. We faced.

"You know, I see the beginning of understanding out her. Patience. Character. Universal and cosmic truths. What do you see?"

Her response was a kiss, deep and brutal filled with viscid passion. I stayed with her, reacting to her touch, her smell and the humidity. "Could you define that", I asked, trying to speak with two tongues.

I pulled away and continued. "You know, Buddhist mother fuckers look at the world as a concept of infinite compassion. People like me are called recluse's. They say we are thorough in in the peaceful life, thorough in good actions, thorough in meritorious conduct and thorough in kindness to all creatures."

The rain was next, over-zealously saturated with shorn content. It was kind of funny, seeing that as a child, I was taught that when it rained while the sun was shining, that the devil was beating his wife. Her damp silk top melted in my palms as if it was wet tissue paper. With her precipitous and profound nipples gasping for air, I positioned her against the car and tasted along the intersection of her breast. My hand freely explored her eloquence as I verged myself closer to her rivalry with all my vigor.

She located my stick, and clawed at my zipper. Her skirt was weighted with water and stuck to my pants, bringing to front an odd sensation of friction and mush. And with one hand, it was brought up to hip-level. I pushed her knee back and let one leg out of the protective dominion of her underwear. Now the dainty silk garments were wet, dangling at the lower part of her right ankle. She pulled my stiffness closer to her, creating a mild blemish of discomfort. I entered.

I could only smell the inert dankness of her hair as it cluttered both my mouth and nose. I rotated impetuously, adding unexpected jolts of pressure whenever it felt as if I could tunnel no further, or when I wanted to hear her speak subconscious French phrases and moans into my ears. As the humidity thickened and with the sun scantly showing itself between the clouds, and the rain drumming a cadence on my car, I found myself unable to control my efforts. She was using the windshield to create more force and more delectable sounds. Again I chewed around her ears, accidently taking into my mouth, one of her earrings.

Before our moment was complete, she allowed me to lift her up off of the auto and position her directly on my structure. Her domineering effusion overwhelmed my resistance, as the prominent forces of mother nature settled me with her choice elixir.

CHAPTER 5
CREATIVITY

"Jimmi, I think that we got a real problem with this Gash Love fellow. He's been seeing an awful lot of your sister."

"I think that those are the words of a defeated man. Give up, she's just a woman, even if she is my sister. She has a life of her own to live. You know?"

"That's not the issue. She doesn't even proclaim the same proudness for her job that she used to. Things are getting out of pocket and I plan to do some research on the subject. I don't like him."

"You don't even know him."

"Hummph!"

"Just don't leave your doors open if you don't want rats on the inside of your house."

"What does he do?"

"Robert, can't you see that I'm occupied. Conduct your research."

Eight months had come and pass since that crisp September night when I first saw Margarita. All of my thought about her seemed to carry me through some type of sentimental backwash. I had pleasured her intimacy and valued it more than just another fiasco of moans and thrust. The vivid remembrance of stroking her into the broken air, with all of my weight, in the rain, made me sweat in eerie silence. Every time I recalled of it, I thought about that old saying, "the devil is beating his wife." The sun and rain you know.

Somewhere between the drinking of the morning and the drinking of the afternoon, I found myself preoccupied with the local tabloids version of the Michael Jordan story. It bored me extremely.

Let's see, if I were to write a story about Michael Jordan, I'd start out in Greece--better yet, Egypt since they stole the ideals for their Gods from there too.

Well, I guess that I'd better say in Greece for all practical purposes, after all, they did get away with the crime of the era.

Back to Mister Jordan. Basketball had to start out over there. So it would read, first of all "and he shall be named Jordan, the God, deity supreme of Basketball." He would sit forty eight inches above Zeus and could never be fucked with. Compliments of his zestful athletic manifestation of course. So much for the sports page.

I had often compared my lifestyle similar to that of one *Peter Camenzind*, and though of my singing abilities as being comparable to, or greater than, Prince or at least David Lee Roth. But, Peter more so than the latter two misfits. In Peter's inoculable world, from his family to his first close associate, mimicked the whole way I lived. Like a constant and infinite struggle in the land of "gonna be". I too, have, and will retain a youthful character throughout my existence. About his writing habits, I can relate to most.

> "With some embarrassment I began composing a few poems, and gradually several notebooks filled up with verse, sketches, and short stories . . . . They were worth little but they made my heart beat faster and filled me with ecstasy."

This was me, almost to the root. But it was only a fraction, a fragmented portion of my ecstatic heart beats. So many other varied parts of my identity comprised my level of self-worth. And basketball was one of them.

Fontain, Tony, and Leon were supposed to be coming by to check out game seven of the Boston/ Detroit series.

My hopes for seeing a Laker/ Bucks final had been desecrated by yours truly, the Boston Celtics. I hate the Celtics. By some kind of means, I always associate them with the ruling an outdated mother fuckers that occupied and chaired the extant list of editorships and review boards that find it more revealing to reject my pieces than to accept them. Both were like a culture that inculcated its citizens to believe that contemplations concerning the future, and success, were fruitless, because their ultimate outcome was left in the hands of the Gods. Yes fruitless, as if all editors wore green and white and owned a summer home in Boston. It's amazing what one tiny article on Michael Jordan can do for the psyche. Expansion, we're talking expansion. Eventually, the sports section was crumpled-up and expanded through the air to the nearest waste container.

The unblushing sounds of the garbage men pricked by, occurring at about the same time the sun chose to rip through the plexi-glass and blinds, grudging the domain of my micro as if it was its solitary obligation. I stumbled over a fervid pile of soiled clothes in an effort to boot the power director.

DING. DONG.

The doorbell. I screamed to the middle of my lungs, "Come in."

It was Willie and Tony. Tony was in the business with me. He was about six feet, 195 pounds and always presented to the public, a weekly delineated fade. He played college football for somebody as quarterback, and broke a plenty of school records. A few white guys on the team found it practical to write on his dormitory door one night:

QUARTERBACK AIN'T A NIGGER POSITION.

He caught them and I tell you, to make a long story brief, it is amazing what two hands and a hammer can do to three mother fuckers.

He got kicked out of school, but he was drafted, in the third round by the Raiders. But only under the title of tail-back/ split-end.

They entered with ceremonial sharpness, extending me their best, most representative slaps of five. In their arms were brown packages of what I anticipated to hold the finest in imported beer. Birra Raffo.

41

Asahi Draft. Red Stripe. Bull. Whatever they were holding, most likely represented some Arabic figure; a fifth, a six, or a twelve.

"What's up?" They wondered.

"The cost of living and a chance of dying." I returned.

"Good mother fucker. Next, we'll have you doing Kotex commercials. Put some clothes on bitch, we don't want to look at your ass!" Leon stated, with a Kool Mild dangling from his lips.

"Why ya'll over here so early?" I questioned with no clothes on, holding my dick.

"Mother fucker, it's 2:15 PM."

He was an artist. He called himself and expiring artist. I could never exactly comprehend why, considering that his talent had been with him ever since he could capture an image with his eyes, and hold a crayon affixed between his fingers. In my apartment, planted aside my bookshelves were oils and water colors that he had created in honor of each of the six books that had been copyrighted in my name. I was his greatest critic and admirer, and there existed no accolade to exhibit my penchant for his works other than bestowing upon him the pleasure of designing each cover for every book I wrote.

Tony followed suit. He put his offering into the ice box and stated. "Yea. Put some clothes on an cut off that freaking computer. . . . Where's the remote? The game will be on in a few. I hope everybody in the garden blow-up on the next space shuttle."

We laughed.

"Tony, you can come back to Earth now." I retorted.

"If I didn't know yo' ass, I think that you were a Boston fan."

Willie went straight to the telephone. He was one of the few associates of mine who could just sit on the phone, and talk to a babe all night. Even if he was not getting any sex from slim. But beside that fatal flaw, he was down and still my boy.

By the end of the first quarter, Fontain had arrived, both teams were blazing from the field, scoring plenty of points and Boston had been called everything, including a child of God. To be honest, I guess that the only thing worse than the Celtics and Larry Bird, was a Celtic fan. The commentators, whoever they were, even though I do recall their names, were tripping, were boring and all on Mr. Bird's dick. Don't get me wrong, I know that people take things-- especially words, out of context. Larry is a great individual talent, but he's just another average basketball player. He just so happens to be 6'9", I'd be some fire too. So we all sat there, looking at the game and just listening. I sat out an eight ball and a tray of some prime-grade bud. I relaxed and they enjoyed.

Then I started thinking deeply. Real deep. Thinking how it would be if they let me and Leon, or anybody I know, commentate a NBA game. . . . Yes, NBA game. Day dreaming is the shit.

"Well Leon, looks like today's game is it. What do you think about the series thus far?"

"Well Gash, let me put it this way. So far it's been what I expected. I would like to see a few more fights. That would make things a lot more interesting."

"Looks like Isiah gonna be penetrating the lanes all day and them Rodman and Salley kids got some leaps."

"Yea, they some real high jumping mother fuckers."

"Man, did you see that slam?" The sound of repetitive slaps of palms are heard.

"That mother fucker is bad, he just came down the court, took off, wet his finger and stuck it in the air for wind direction and bolted that mother fucker."

"If that mother fucking Ainge foul him like that again, they gonna be throwing blows up in here."

"These refs are fucked up. They ain't calling no fouls on them Irish niggers."

Yea, and Boston been playing 2-1-2 the entire game. What's up with that?"

43

"Fuck this shit man, these mother fuckers finna win. At the half, let's go to the truck and burn one up."

"I'm down. My computer recording the shit anyway."

"Give me a beat man."

"We can't rap on the air."

"Why not? We each got a microphone. We'd turn it out. We'd be live. The audience, they chilled, they chilled. We listen to music when we run ball don't we?"

"Yea, but let's jus' cool on out and see if we can get the camera men to get some views of the dancers and the babes in the crowd."

"I'd go for that."

"Don't forget to contact me when I get my franchise."

"Smell the coffee, Blacks don't own sports teams, not even amateur ones. We just play on them. Where would they be anyway?"

"In Vancouver. Yea, the Vancouver Pimps. I'll keep you in mind for G.M."

"Right! You big trying to have an NBA team in a hockey city type mother fucker."

Gash! Yo black, what you trippin on this time? Willie questioned, bringing me outside of my fantastic capsule of make-believe.

"You thinking about Miss Fine, ain't ya?" He questioned, passing me the joint.

"I wasn't thinking about slim. I was waiting for you to light that joint." I opined, rubbing my hands across the carpet.

"Ain't no matches, them were the last." Willie responded.

I tossed him an azure colored lighter and remarked. "We got an extreme heat making machine right there, courtesy of Bic."

I had tried desperately, in artless disgust it appears, to loosen the collectivism that Margarita and I had established. She had approached the point of trying to read everything that I produced. First, it started

out with a play. Next, a book of poems and then finally, short stories. She thought that all of my main characters represented some unconscious parody of my
constructs, as if through them, my selection between
fear and confidence was delivered. When she read
them, an edge of anxiety leaked under her smile, making her expand and glow with something more than
delusion. Even when our sheer mechanics provided
the precious heat of intercourse, it was not uncommon
of her to refer to me as one of my protagonist.

In one since, it was a thrill, it awarded me the
respect of the rapture, as if all of my "non-heroes" had
individually, spoken words of love to her. When we
were together, I felt as if I wanted to discover something new, everywhere I looked. Her gorgeous exhibi-
tionism, the way in which she glided her lips across
mine, all were retrospective of our evenings, in piano
bars, quiet grills and under moons. She was the kind
of person that, if she could, she would have kept the
sun shimmering, all year long, in an effort to keep the
afternoons that we spent at the lake view.

The others quickly reminded me however, of the
impending result of the game. Boston won. But what
can you expect from a simple-minded nigger that
thinks himself to exhibit the style of a man of letters? It
was only proper that my team did not win. What was
new? I like the rest of my innocent collaboration of
street-loyal scholars, as did myself, considered it--the
game, to be a sporting event, even if it was played on a
parquet floor. Economic? No way.

We were heart broken until we remembered that
they would now have to face the Lakers. The thought
alone initiated an overwhelmingly, positive effect in us.

"They can't fuck with LA." Willie chanted with
his fist clenched tightly in the air.

"Where ya going?" I questioned.

"In the back for a minute."

"You big on the phone, all night long type mother fucker. You ain't foolin' nobody." Tony yelled.

Willie came back into the room to defend his honor.

"Can't a cat jus' talk on the phone with out getting checked up in this mother fucker? Now I ask you, the humble members of the jury, is it a crime for a nigger to take advantage of cable optics, when so conveniently supplied?"

By now the remote was in Leon's hands and was no sooner clicked to wrestling. And another subject would manifest.

"Them some big mother fuckers." Tony remarked, finishing off a Red Stripe.

"And they can dance too." I added.

"And act." Willie punctuated.

"He's like,. . . I'm having my way with this mother fucker." Fontain commented, kicking off his shoes.

"Jones ruthless!" Willie exclaimed.

"You know he makes money, he's mean and uses salt." I added.

"And weighs 350 pounds." Willie punctuated. This time, going a step further in his commentary." You know niggers love to hate him."

"He's hazing homeboy." Leon phrased, with his eyes sternly jointed to the optic emissions of the cathode ray tube.

"Boom!" Tony blurted as one of the giants jumped off of the top rope on the other dudes neck, with his knee cap.

"Elbow drop." Fontain called as the next maneuver suddenly had flourished into the land of past tense.

"Ahhhhhhh." We all sighed in chorus, as the pile driver rested the subject in the middle of the ring.

The mean jones then ended it. This time it was for real. As he raised his victim in exegetical congruence, displaying him somberly as if it was rehearsed, out on to the concrete.

"There ya' go." I extended, giving out fives at random.

46

"Percussive skull bongo." Tony yelled taking the majority of my fives.

It was hard to discern the actual direction of the evening's carousal. Tony was seen as the single remainder of our cactus. Every light was on, every blind closed. I had seen as a child, on some government program pertaining to surveillance, that it was possible, electronically, to record with minor distortion, an entire conversation from 300 yards away, through the windows. It made sense to me at the time and still does.

And for precautionary measures, tiny Bose speakers were posted beside every window. Eleven total. They "sounded" good too.

Tony never flinched or exhibited any emotionalism affiliated with timidity and fear. If it had been left up to me to single out one word in an attempt to capture his existence, the word that I would select would be HARD. He use to always talk about the time he told a scout representing the Bengals that he'd "run into a brick wall if they paid him enough."

Sometimes, it was hard to perceive, that although he was impervious to furtive embarrassment, he could allow himself to be swallowed up by the enchanted sounds of Micheal Franks. I could tell that something was on this mind, and that he did not know exactly how to proceed with the issue.

From the black and white stillness of the album cover, I could tell that his favorite song would soon traduce across my inner ear. With Wilton Felder on bass and Joe Sample on keyboards, and lyrics for the erotic eternal, they comprised to lift my feeling of creative sanctity:

> "THE LADY STICKS TO ME LIKE WHITE ON RICE
> SHE NEVER COOKS THE SAME WAY TWICE--
> MAYBE IT'S THE MUSHROOMS
> MAYBE THE TOMATOES
> I CAN'T REVEAL HER NAME
> BUT EGG PLANT IS HER GAME
> WHEN MY BABY COOKS HER EGGPLANT
> SHE DON'T NEED NO BOOK

AND SHE'S GOT A GIOCONDA
KIND OF DIRTY LOOK. . . .
MAYBE IT'S THE WAY SHE GRATES HER CHEESE
OR JUST THE FRECKLES ON HER KNEES
MAYBE IT'S THE SCALLIONS
MAYBE SHE'S ITALIAN
I CAN'T REVEAL HER NAME
BUT, EGGPLANT IS HER GAME. . . ."

Tony sat in the brightness of the pallid white painted walls, looking weightlessly up at the ceiling, with his head perched atop the sofa and his lips following every word, an eighth of a second off the original pace.

"What are you creating this time?" He asked, sitting up a little bit. "I hope it's not that fine ass French bitch."

"On the contrary. I'm making-up a gangster-Camus type story. based on the Gash Love's construct principle."

"What?"

"Never mind. What up with ya?"

He did not hesitate. "Some people said that this guy came down to the barber shop. Say he was asking questions about you. They say he has a badge."

I continued to press on into the development of my story. The song was suddenly, spawning an eruption of decomposed neglect.

"Put on some Funkedelic, will ya? *Hardcore Jollies*." He obeyed. As the new beat undulated between the past due smell of herb, and the sweet coolness of the lights, Tony continued to insert his position.

"I think we got a real problem. I think that we better cool down after these next few drops."

"We'll see."

"And black, the babe, you been kind of lagging lately."

"Yea, yea, I know. Don't worry so much, will ya Tony,"

I stood up from my desk and embellished myself to maximum protection. I cut off the lights and clicked the remote. Now the notable whiteness that

48

shimmered in the apartment, displayed itself vulnerable to the luminance of the dappled moonlight.

"You ready?" He motioned his head in the affirmative and walked out of the door. "You drive, I got the paper."

I saved my information and went into the kitchen. Christian was still in her nest under the kitchen sink. I kept eight shells in her .20 barrel. I took better care of her nickle-plated, pistol-grip body than I did myself.

CHAPTER 6
SUSPICION

"Hello."

"How do you feel today?"

"Oh, alright. Just got a few things that I need to tie up."

"My bed rings of you. I don't like the smell of men in my bed."

"Oh! But you know that I'm not down with the carpet burn camp."

"Will I see you today?"

"Maybe. Me and Tony got some things to take care of. Maybe after eight."

"I have something that I need to discuss with you."

"What is it? Is it urgent?"

"Not really.....Attends Marie."

"Good. I want to finish reading this book."

"Oh."

A sharp click sound is heard through the phone. "Hold on for a second, please ? I'll be right back."

She did not wait for an answer.

And on the other end.

"Hello."

"How you doing? I missed you for lunch yesterday. Are you O.K.?"

"Yea, I'm on the other line, hold on."

She clicked back.

"Gash., I'll talk with you later. My brother is on the other line. I'll call you in about fifteen."

"Alright, I'll talk to you later."

"I miss you. Bye."

"Hello, I'm back."

"Who was that?"

"Robert that is none of your business."

"Oh yea, well, I'm gonna make it mine. I was talking to your brother about it. I don't think that you should be seeing him. Have you forgotten about that diamond."

"No but things are different now. I want to settle down now, and start a family. I'm sorry, but, it's not you and me. I'm sorry Robert. I must go now. I have a doctor's appointment."

The more I tried to exert my reverent ambitions as a writer, the more hardships surmounted. Sometimes I wretchedly believed that if it had not been for my Apple, I would have allowed these tangled and disorientated clusters of antagonisms to influence me. But I did not.

Blinded, mesmerized by its zealous, geometrical shape, for hours, I would sit, pecking away with two fingers. Creating what me and my friends satirized as being masterpieces of the future. The general assumption was that by 40, I would be great. Sometimes I dreamed of publishing manuscripts under the pseudonym Anti-Climacus, flooding the universe with a gregarious mass of knowledge. Eventually helping others to understand that existence is not given to man, but rather an ideal that one can create individually.

Writing was like sex, a primitive, and beautiful type thing that could only be compared to the titular impressions of the ocean waves against the flesh, or the pulsatory demonstration of a tropical bird of paradise during mating season.

For three days now, I had been awakened by the sun-soaked stillness of a parked taxi cab. Its appearance, humble and malevolent, sparked inside of me, a formidable perplexity. Only in old detective movies, did I affiliate the indented habitation of motor vehicles for periods extending past eight hours.

Turning the cable slowly, shamelessly peeking between the two blinds parted with the assistance of my middle fingers, I looked, almost abhorrently, at the fallacious condition that the object and its occupants purported. The beats were still pumping. For an instant, I removed myself from the window. I went into the study and turned on the stereo. Sometimes, in my mind, I thought that the ubiquitous sounds of music, like for example, the Pat Matheny that was on the radio, made me examine my condition of public life in a more than obtrusive manner. But I was down to listen to no jazz.

I turned on the CD player instead and threw on *'We Can't Be Stopped'*, the Geto Boys new jammy. I clicked to identify the disk number. Five. And the selection, number six. The song, *My Mind Playing Tricks On Me.*

"At night I can't sleep, I toss and turn
candles sticks in the dark,
visions of bodies being burned
four walls just starring at a nigger
I'm paranoid sleeping with my finger on the trigger
My mother always stressing I ain't living right
but I ain't going out without a fight
See every time my eyes close,
I start sweating,
and blood starts coming out my nose
It's somebody watching me act.
But I don't know who it is
so I'm watching my back
I can see um when I deep in the covers
When I awake I don't see the mother fucker
He owns a black hat like I own
A black suit and a cane like my own
Some might say take a chill B
But fuck that shit, there's a nigger trying to kill me
I'm popping in the clip when the wind blows
every twenty seconds
got me peeping out my windows
Investigating the joint for traps
Checking my telephone for taps
I'm starring at the woman on the corner
It's fucked up when your
mind playing tricks on ya."

Margarita had mentioned, every now and then, through her half-twisted smile, hints of wanting to move away. Sometimes she even made it sound as if her plan entailed me as being one of the pieces of luggage. I had written of marriage, and had observed it take from me some of my dearest childhood companions. Indirectly, the situation perturbed me, making my mind journey to near and far places; to Peru and Memphis, to Alaska and the Arabian Gulf, to Danhomey and the reading public.

After a period, my thoughts returned to the moment. I began to reconsider the moderate, possible threat of the establishment that I considered to resemble a police headquarters on wheels. And I recalled of the money. We had not entertained any sort of negotiates with our normal clientele since Tony found out that some people with badges were asking questions about me. We figured it was the smart thing to do. The only incriminating evidence around the cut was thirty-seven thousand dollars that I was going to donate to Monroe in his bid for the position of State Attorney General.

Now it would appear as if I would have to go to the bank. The nearest one was around the corner in this real uppity mall. I really didn't like going there anymore, after Willie Mitch got transferred to the headquarters, downtown. Other than that, the people at the bank were real acceptable, and tendered to the legal nature of the greenback as if it was more important than breast feeding infants. All of the tellers knew my name and the branch manager and I often played golf together. I was one of the very few depositors that was allowed to use a designated employee's parking space. Two of the more "chiseled to perfection", top-heavy tellers had even joined me in the deracination of physical gyration. More astonishing, was the fact that more than sixty percent were dedicated patrons.

Suppurating the efficacy to accost the service attendant, I waved at the security guard -- one of my loyalist consumer -- and gestured to him that it was off-season. He reciprocated the communication with a bleached smile and returned to his duties, aiding an elderly woman out the door. Being a little before one, the majority of the service attendants were making head-way for lunch. I waited until I was recognized. Barbara was the first to free herself.

As usual, I dwelled for a second, disparately, even blatantly at her lower features. I had even de-scribed one of my characters, in a successful purge to collect her temperament, her symmetry, her comely en-campment, after an experience that we had commensu-rated in the safe one rain engendered evening. And none of my boys believed the story.

It started with one story. I gave her one story and she has perceived me as irresistible ever since then. I tell you, the powers of grammar combine with free thinking, are a mother fucker. Especially if a demented and talented, gangster-type mother fucker as myself, represents the previous.

"Gash", she says. "What can I do for you?"

"Just need to get to my box." I said, waiting for her to say something about the last time we spent to-gether.

"Follow me." She said, as her chignon hair-do, with waved bangs near the front accented her bold and gold earrings. Boy do I admire the projection of knit dresses by the well-defined female anatomy.

"I was about to go to lunch", she stated. "Re-member that time when you made me French fries and dirty rice with ground Turkey for lunch. It was the first time I saw you."

"Well, If you wait a minute, we can go some-where together."

She smiled. I'm so nice.

Barbara had always displayed her person in a method which made her resemble a temptress of fash-ion to all whomever laid eyes on her. I waited outside, in the mall portion of the plaza, looking around at the various differences presented by the general public. Near the drug store, was an elderly couple, sitting on a bench tending to the beastly needs of a five year-old and her ice cream cone. Exiting the Lord and Taylor, was a young man and his female companion. He was evidently exhausted from his detail in the shoe section for I could discern a slight bit of animosity in his eyes whenever she would stop to examine the window displays. By the time that he had noticed the less than thrilling gaze that I was directing at his date, he held his position, looking dishonestly at a cramping window of assorted colored pumps and sandals. Do not get me wrong, I was looking at the young woman contemptuously, however, she was short, and I on the other hand, was tall enough to thump her on the head and kill her instantly.

Barbara and I walked, innocently, to the nearest restaurant. She jumped to disagree with my selection of this Korean joint because it served dried fish for an appetizer. And she knew that I would seek my fill, while at the same time, telling stories about this guy I knew who was into barb-q goldfish. I say this in reference to the fact that if you are into eating dried fish, the next time the opportunity confronts you, see if it kind of reminds you of barb-q.

The openness of the mall, the florid excrescence of the plants, the glass, the sun, and the canorous clattering of a thousand tongues, contrived to enhance my vision with an almost stupefying trance. It was her, Margarita, wearing with passive accretion, a strapless black and white polka-dot dress. One could see a skimp of erotism in her smile, a jealous contention in her brow, and a dash of desire in her amorous charcoal black eyes.

When she noticed us, at first, she looked at me as if I was a first cousin, once removed. And then, with a sigh of relief, as if the thought of the size of my sex had suddenly entered her mind. Barbara's presence had become as independent as the entire universe and thoughts of unearned sex with her, during her lunch hour, had quickly dissipated from my mental sphere. And although I was no proponent of displaying emotional sentiment in public, in no other form than the laugh, I allowed her to greet me in her usual firm and fulgurous[16] way.

I stood back. "Barbara, I would like to introduce you to Miss Margarita Fine. Miss Fine, Barbara Dallas."

They exchanged opening remarks and tributes of the other's attire, almost as if they were two fighters prior to the ringing of the bell indicating the start of round one. Then their innate Sybil or S.B.I.O.[17] personality traits emerged.

Margarita threw the first punch, a right uppercut. "Miss Dallas, you carry yourself well for your age."

Barbara returned with a left hook. "Oh yes. I stopped wearing a training bra some years ago, but you wouldn't know about such progression."

"It's a beautiful day", I threw out, lacking only a bow-tie, a stiffly starched white shirt, and sanctioned approval from the WBC.

As their volley of words evinced an ending, Barbara finally offered to escort her to the ladies room to help her with her make-up. Since there were now, ten minutes remaining of her lunch period, I told her to call me and watched her as she entered the somnolent quarters of that Korean restaurant that served free, dried fish.

I escorted Margarita to her vehicle.

"Who was she? Kind of old don't you think? She has to be at least forty."

"She's just a friend", I returned."

"She likes you a lot, doesn't she?"

"Na, I doubt it. She just likes to spend money on me, and likes to give the services of her mouth to me. While I'm at the drive thru, of course."

"I know the story. She meets a nigger like you and falls madly, head-over-heels in love with you. She desires and craves every moment she sees you, talks to you and thinks of you. You should be very honored."

---

[16] Emitting flashes of light.
[17] Sixteen bitches in one .

57

"O.K., so I'm a judge."

"And there's another side", she opined. "She admires you, yes admires you, and your creative disposition for the absurd and the realness apart of your every action. She likes it when you tell her to meet you behind a building on her lunch break. She likes the feeling of being held in the arms of a man who would be down for having sex all day. Bringing you some food, some beer, or some computer paper, in exchange for your disingenuous and immensely delicate libido."

"So, are you making an order of any of the side dishes mentioned above?" I asked.

"Finissons la leson." I did not know what it meant, but it sure sounded good to me at the time.

She followed me home.

The taxi was still in the same position as I closed the door of my auto, waiting and finally watching Margarita pull into my driveway. We went inside. Her mission was straight forward and directed towards the couch. Within an hour she was gone. She had learned to boot my computer. The message she left read:

THE POWER YOU GIVE ME IS PERMANENT.

For a moment, it confused my drained senses. I was, at the instant, like Clerimont and "could stand no noise except for the sound of (my) own voice". Amid signs of discomfort, I found shelter in an one act play I was working on entitled "AS THE STOICS PUT IT".

One of the characters in the three scene, one act play was a detective. He was the sort of fellow that extended and confused, the conflicts and happenings of his family activity, with the fostered operations of his lawful duties. I made him almost like Robert. He was unable to establish a sense of stability, personality wise, and the ability to decenter anything related to him, was irreversibly restricted, to the concrete experiences of his fiscal, and egocentric acclaim. It would not faze me a bit if the people who have been watching me lately, were some of his Department of Justice serfs.

I could understand how his distorted desire to inject his perception into the minds of others manifested. Prestigious boarding schools' since age six, Yale, Phi Beta Kappa and John F. Kennedy School of Law. I had a friend just like that when I was growing up. He went to private, university level schools all of his life -- in which he was the only bro of African descent. He used to tell me that the only way that he could cool out was by eating his lunch with the cafeteria workers and the janitorial staff; since they were the only ones whom he could joke, curse and laugh, and whom would respect and listen to him and hear what he had to say, no matter how miniscule it was or appeared to be. Now, all he does is pretends as if he is still at Stanford, rant and rave about commodities and expect to receive slaps of five every time he smiles, or utters a single word. Yes, the white man did him in. Just like he did in at least 100 million more of my kind these past years. Not including the herds and flocks of millions that died during the midway's passage -- 'ey. I'd say about 20 million -- take that descendants of the holocaust victims. You got to listen because I've been forced a many of nights, to watch billions of concentration camp and Hitler movies. And you know what, no telling how many he will do in with the future right next door. I just hope that I will not be one of them. I will always keep my mind, and my ability to write. No one will be able to take that away from me. Nobody.

The darkness had come quickly, even with daylight saving time on her side. I had been putting in the front room for nearly twenty minutes. I was concentrating on every putt. My eyes looked down that antiquated brown, wood-aluminun shaft, and frequently, to the prepared target of eighteen feet away. In the background, were the loud, very loud and ubiquitous sounds of Doug E Fresh & The Get Fresh Crew - *Play This Only At Night*. All I worried about was the beat. It had to be desperate and suicidal, pulsating and head-moving, creative and cantabile, while at the same time, tender enough to be appreciated as a classically contrived piece of art.

There was a movie out when I graduated from college called PHANTASM. A-1 flick. Well, to make my point, the musical theme of that movie sounded just like the music of this Doug E. Fresh song. The only difference was the addition of a beat. I could have listened to it all night, putted forever.

I pretended that I was in competition. Probably at The Olympic Club or somewhere in Europe. I was on the green in two, dog-leg to the left, par four. My flight included Judith Krantz, Louis L'Amour and this young Jamaican guy that I had never heard of before. We were playing sudden death for the Pulitzer. How Ms. Krantz survived the four rounds, I will never know. Needless to mention, she hit her first ball into the lake and her second into a garbage can. It finally boiled down to me and the Jamaican chap.

That Doug E. Fresh cut, or Theme from PHANTASM music was breaking vividly, though the tinseled audience of people and Spruce. I glanced at the pin and Saw that Robert, outlined in black, was tending it. However, his size fourteen wingtips were in the way. I waited until he moved his foot. And when he did, this little, tiny metallic object, with spinning blades and tees, flew directly at me.

I missed the put, I lost the prize and I woke up.

The music continued to vibrate through the conjecture of my humble dwelling.

I try to run but I can not. It is as if everything has slowed down to a snails pace. I begin to stand, my door is kicked in. They stand tall, I represent nothing weak. I will fight to the death -- an issue of ontological necessity.

Both blond and plus two-hundred pounds. The bearded-one orders a double-fist, baseball-swing, upper-cut to the chin. There goes my turntable. The other, suggested that I add a straight right to the side of my head, to the menu. I considered his advice and proposed that he reconsider and order the knee to the jewels and knee to the chin special. I even threw in a kick to the stomach. It was fun while It lasted.

Where am I? This does not look like any place official. I guess bearded shorty clucked me with his automatic. Isshhhha, I won't touch it any more. I wonder if they fixed my door? They did not show me a warrant.

The lights hung poetically, looming above the vacant darkness of what seemed to be a cheap motel room. I could hear of no cars, reminding me that my position had to be anywhere other than a major thoroughfare. The hairy fellow displayed a large gash aside his chin, with a tap of blood dried beneath his nasal cavity. He was positioned on top the chester drawer, picking at his sore, causing a trickle of blood to appear.

"Where am I?" I questioned impatiently.

"Shut the fuck up and wait!" He exclaimed, as if I had damaged his person. It was his lack of adroitness that caused him to bang his head on my turntable.

"I have the right to know, you know?"

Brashly he opined, "Well, excuse my ignorance."

"Well, if it's alright for you, it's alright for me." I laughed. He slapped me. And I spat in his face. A good and juicy spit with air bubbles and white foam. Then, I thought to myself, of my situation, of my immediate circumstances. I reminded myself of this poem that I once recited in a third grade play that my teacher had written about some race riot in the first decade of the century. It was by Claude McKay.

> If we must die - let it not be like hogs
> Hunted and penned in an inglorious spot,
> While round us bark the mad and hungry dogs.
> Making their mock at our accursed lot.
> If we must die--oh let us nobly die,
> So that our precious blood may not be shed
> In vain; then even the monsters we defy
> Shall be constrained to honor us though dead!
> Oh, Kinsmen! We must meet the common foe;
> Though far out numbered, let us show us brave
> And for their thousand blows deal one death blow

What though before us lies the open grave?
Like men we'll face the murderous, cowardly pack
Pressed on the wall, dying but fighting back!

I thought that they clapped for me because they knew that I had worked over time to memorize it. It has been with me every since. I did not know what it meant, until some friends of mine were ambushed on a subway by this white man who was in law school at the time.

The rumble of laughter and the slapping of leather heels against the outside walkway stirred my attention. I thought no more of the poem, but it was with me inductively. I knew that it had to be Robert.

He walked in, quickly grinning his well-groomed grin. Unbuttoning the top button of his suit, opening his vest, expanding to my vision, that ugly, brown and red tie.

"Nice tie." I commented.

"Thank you mister Love, thank you." He paused, locked the door and continued. " So we meet at last. Sounds like a movie don't it?"

"I would disagree but it's really not germane. I've seen you before. You've seen me before, I've seen you before. Cut the bull shit, we both know what's up."

"My aids tell me that you were unwilling to listen to negotiation."

I looked at both carefully. "Do they talk?"

"You should have not resisted."

"Resistance, negotiation? What negotiations? If two big ass, hair-on-the back, WASP-type mother fuckers kicked your door down you'd throw blows too!

"Alright mister Love, enough then of this, as you say, bull shit."

"But first, can you un tie me. Your boy over there got 357 reasons to keep me from leaving."

He looked at me, and then back to the other chap, who had entered with him. He pulled his pants up, revealing the lazy efforts of his hose, and pulled up a chair besides me. A head motion was the signal to release me. I gazed downward, at the cheap, dingy, and villainous emerald green carpet; that if closely examined, displayed minute particles of sand.

I tasted both wrist with my hands. My right baby finger was swollen and rigid.

"Well mister Love. Hummmm, summa cum laude. Impressive. Now, you can do better than dropping out of medical school. I hear Meharry isn't that difficult."

"So I guess you heard wrong."

"Well, I guess that I heard wrong about your underground business activities."

A large question marked entered my mind. I did not know exactly, what to expect, what he was talking about. But I knew that if he had anything legitimate, that I would be in the pen for at least four presidents. With dauntless bearings, I looked into the ceramic suavity of his eyes. Pulling the insides of my jaws together tighter, preparing them to pronounce my next remarks.

I had nothing against him, but then again I do not look at six million dollar man re-runs either. He walked around the room, surprisingly calm, carrying on like the kind of gentleman that would select R.C. over Coke, or gingerale over Gatorade.

"I'd feel a bit more cooled out if you let your pets out for a leak."

He returned with yet another head motion.

"Wait." he suddenly threw out. "You two stay here, me and our friend are going for a ride."

Was he into classic movies or what? I mean, he is almost as bad as me, with my day dreaming.

He continued. "It's that alright with you mister Love?"

I nodded my head in the affirmative.

It was funny to hear that what old boy had collected on me had nothing to do with the business. I took it as a compliment. Get this, some political essays that I had written some twelve years before, from his perspective, were grounds enough to send me away on

63

the McCarren-Walter Act of 1952. I, barely myself, was familiar with it. But it works to "exclude a number of writers and thinkers from leaving this country because of ideological beliefs evidenced in their writings". I was very tired and sore. My baby finger was hurting more than anything. He rambled on incoherently while I camouflaged my impending state of rapid eye movements. I could sleep a little better now knowing on the inside that I was not gonna be nailed by the I.R.S. or on charges of intent to distribute narcotic substances -- even though we all know that a narcotic substance is operationally defined as any substance of an opium derivative.

He stopped the auto at Margarita's apartment. She stayed there when she wanted to exclude her self from the celebrated auspices of her brother. He opened my door and slung me brutally, by the throat, on to the sidewalk. I felt a bone snap in my wrist, sounding louder than his violent slamming of the door. He noticed that I was holding my wrist and kicked me in it, ordering me to get up and walk to the door. I obeyed.

He had proven himself to me, to be no more different from the two white men that he had sent to address me earlier. It seemed as if he thrived off of power, as if he lived for simple control, relegating all other than himself, and all subject to his manipulation, as subordinate objects merely designed to entertain and stimulate his temper.

I rang the door bell. I waited. Through the glass pane adjacent to the door, I could detect her silhouette flaunting towards our position. She opened the door.

In the past, I had prided myself on my level of self-control and my uncanny ability to cover all glimpse of apprehension whenever I was stressed, or perceived myself to be in an unprecedented situation. However, I was hurting bad and unable to hide it from her. He shoved me inside but this time I did not fall. I still was holding my hand, and my pinky was now in excruciating pain.

A confused guise developed in her eyes. "Robert, Gash, what is the meaning of this?" She questioned, apparently astonished at our assemblage.

"I looked around, at Robert, at her, at Robert again. I was still paying close attention to my hand.

I answered,"according to your friend and mines, I'm a political prisoner. I write propaganda against the government he says. He full of shit!"

He kicked me in the leg, this time pulling out a small, seemingly nickle-plated Glock 17.

"Robert, stop it. What is wrong with you?"

She accosted him verbally, relinquishing a spirit comparable to that of a cyclone. And in return, he gave his imitation of a natural, wind contrived disaster. Blowing into the area of her face with dull esteem.

"Don't act as if there is nothing wrong. I should have never trusted you with my heart. And , and, all the things that I ever gave you, besides myself." Robert stated, pronouncing each word as if it was coming from the mouth of another individual.

Margarita looked up in the air, partly prattled and partly debilitated. She appeared as if she did not know what was going on in the inside of herself, like our combined presence, in conjunction with the blue abode of the room, made her litigious to punishment.

"What do you mean? Honestly", she retorted to the top of her lungs, looking up at the ceiling for a moment. "I don't understand you. I simply don't. And I seriously doubt if the patience will return to me, that will make me understand your actions."

"You lie, you have always lied. You do not think of me you worthless whore."

Now, I considered myself to represent the sleazy, impassionate type. However, unlike Robert, I have never, to this day, lowered myself to the order of beating on dames -- unless it was in self-defense, or in other words, if they attacked me with a knife and threaten to kill me if I ever left them. However, she made no offensive effort to strike him.

"Tell, him about your little visit to the doctor. What was it for? We'd all, like to know." He demanded, folding his arms as if he was in Kindergarten, and had answered a question correctly.

"Tell him!" he exclaimed to the peak of his voice." Tell him, tell us both. Tell us about your pregnancy, you cheap half-breed."

I saw him hit her in the face again. Slapping her in the mouth with a veneered backhand. I do not know if it was the suggestion of him hitting her, or if it was the fact that his back was turned, or if it was the observation that he had used the pistol as a provincial instrument, that made me smash him over the head with a black and white portable television set. It had been conveniently situated on the dividing counter disuniting the kitchen from the major edifice. And I made sure to kick him in the head four times, one for each blow that I had junctured to trawl in care of his extremities.

CHAPTER 7
RETROSPECT

Of that granular night, I could only recall of the ill-starred night, traversing over pot-hole after pot-hole, and of the round, abscond and esoteric pulsations of the sounds emanating through the radio.

I did not know if it was a tape, or if it was coming from some simple-minded mass communication network. Even though it was not of grand importance to me, it did take my illusive mind from my paining finger and my protruded wrist. As it stands now, the out-spoken beats, as they were then, are just as fresh and soothing to my ethereal spirit. Club Nouveau. *Why You Treat Me So Bad.*

Margarita was singing along, sensitively dedicating her every breath to it, as if she were its mistress. An evaporated pattern of stars roared along the gunny visionary medium of the windshield, as my jounced head rested adeptly in her lap.

After a while, only the pluperfect and incessant bass beat of the song collected my attention. Dump-dump, dump-dump. Dump-dump, dump. Eight note, eight note. Eight note, quarter note-rest. Down-up, down-up. Down-up, down-rest. Ghetto Bass. That is all that I could think of. I was even void of the experience of day dreaming.

It was indeed a different perspective to be looked upon, why she held from me the fact that she was with child? But more so than that, the difference was buried in the issue of life. I had cultured something in vitro. It was part of me. And with a little luck, it would look, or at least have some feature that was characteristic of me. Boy or girl, made no never mind.

Where we were was of minor importance. There was a large body of water nearby, but very few people. The sun appeared to be consistent with my beliefs, bringing with its beams, pretentious hopes of creative thought. And there were trees, magnificent and gracious trees that covered the area as if mold cultivating on wheat bread.

She never told me completely what happened that night. But she did tell me that the reason that I was minus the physical stamina to enter the car those five months ago was because she had hit me over the head with Robert's pistol. I really did not expect her to tell me that I had actually killed Robert. I tried to kill him and I was more than self-assured and confident, that any activity that I am willing to start, that It would be carried out to the fullest. After the television, there was really no need to kick him the way I did. But I did and I was not ashamed of it.

There used to be a time in shit, when I was growing up, when everybody knew that there were no rules in fighting. There was no official or referee and it seemed as if the only individuals that understood this were the best fighters -- by best, I am referring to those fighters anti of the professional ranks who exhibit a delicate penchant for winning at any cost. Shit, everybody that I hung around with knew that it was okie dokie to pop a mother fucker in the back of the head, or shoot them in the back before they turned around and shot you. Common sense. Just like knowing that Harper Lee's *To Kill a Mockingbird* was rejected by publishers almost as many times as James Cain's *The Postman Always Rings Twice.* Authorities say that Mr. Cain's novel was rejected so many times that the "postman rang twice" each day.

In two months we would be parents. The doctors, with the aid of ultrasound, concluded that the offspring would be a girl.

I had not been writing as much as I had used to and it seemed that the last time I touched a computer was fifty light years ago. I did not consider this to be a problem. The trees, the sun and the lake alone filled me with enough free thought to question the initial purpose of my physical existence.

I enjoyed Margarita's presence and thought of her in periods in which I wanted to see the baby. Sometimes I would even wish that I could make it come out immediately, so that I could hold and squeeze that which was a manifestation of my genetic code. I used to consider myself sterile.

I had never gotten a woman pregnant and often contributed this phenomena to my extant preference for the consumption of a certain relative of both the oat and radish. But the stubborn reality of the entire issue rested in my giddy ability to procreate.

I had created things, places, events, people, violence, emotion and humor, in my previous years with the somber assistance of the twenty-six alphabets and my creative philology. I never started writing for fame, or money, or avarice or recognition, but because it seems as if, like the rotating of the earth around the sun, that it was what I was prescribed to do. It was what I did and I could not obviate the sedulous level of seriousness that I had on numerous times, awarded to it. I did not know if I did it to escape, but I doubt it. It was more than an escape, it was just like making a baby in many respects. However, there did exist bland and slender differences, mostly which centered around the sexual medium required.

But getting back to where we were, we were occupying a spastic, little dwelling that belonged to her cousins. I had never seen them, but I was frequently reinforced to the fact that they were somewhere near. And if their assistance was needed for emergency and or precautionary measures, Margarita need not travel no further than the kitchen telephone.

She had been sleep all day it seemed. The sovereign spawn of the wind had recycled itself with an aloofness that I had previously observed only in the way newspapers were flung at the door step by passing couriers. She rested so palliative, moving every now and then, in an anent[18] manner that would cover

---

[18] Along side with; Leveled.

her polished toe nails with the extreme ends of the covers. The annular swelling of her abdominal cavity reminded me of the time my youngest baby sister had been born.

My whole family had been in serious attendance at that Baptist hospital. There were few, if any people around that day. The halls were marked with passionate hues of grey and blue, and the air flooded with antiseptic. Giant panes of glass lined one side while the steepness of drink machines rested opposites as their mates. I recall jumping down the vast area, avoiding the large diamonds that encapsulated the smaller ones located in the very center of the arranged tile. I almost ran into a doctor not paying attention to where I was looking.

All day, I had decided it my egocentric privilege, to dispose of accumulated intestinal gases. When the nurse first brought out the baby, I was somewhere near the obscurity of the emergency room. I came back and they said it was behind the huge glass window. I picked her out immediately. And now, I had expected the circumstances to manifest the same for our offspring.

I respect Margarita and I respect her a plenty. But people, somehow, always seem to perceive me as some sort of a tyrant gigolo. As if I was not capable of sharing my existence with others completely, in specific other of the opposite gender. Just because the Snow White, Valentino, Lutheran motif, was not present in my exiled future, past or present. I believed in self-determination to the fullest extent, and practiced what I preached on occasions. However, it appeared as if all of that would change; I was content, about to become a real-live father, and could document the fluent exposition on paper.

There was in the vacuity of the cabin, a miniature, antiquated, black typewriter. It sat in the corner of the kitchen, behind a stack of newspapers adjacent to the pantry. It reminded me of one that I had seen on this cover of a collection of selected poems by Langston Hughes.

The anomalous feeling it aroused inside of me was extremely different than the one that I experienced when I woke up in front of my desk top. The urge was not there. I could not turn it on and there existed no monitor to look up on and make corrections. If I needed to edit, there existed no control command to change the aberrant deformation of the cursor, just another page was pulled from the stack and more bottles of Liquid Paper depleted.

One day, there was the augurous[19] urge to write down some reflections concerning this little duck I saw get run over by a speed boat. The image was so fiendish that the first thought that came to mind was one of innovation. I thought to myself of emotion. The emotion that I attributed to the greedy habits of the crippled and the frightened. The frivolous handicaps of the economic disadvantaged. The simple conundrums of an organized and single kind. I thought that a mother fucker who would run over a duck, and not demonstrate the will or desire to slow down, was a raucous and low-down mother fucker. The kind that would marry for money or care more for material accumulation than philanthropic necessity. But who was I to make such a judgement? I figured that I was just as bad.

I had not totally considered the mental adjustments that I would be forced to make, learning to live with another. It would be completely different now, with the diffuse emptiness of space that so many times aided me in my fantastic treks to the non-conscious, distorted, by the presence of a woman. A creature of such hood-winking pleasure, flooded with so much comparison, so much, that one song could not describe her and one rainbow did an injustice to her. Her company brought to my attention, all that I had imagined

---

19 p
Like a prognostication.

and expected of a babe. She was the shit and that sexy ass French accent was some fire too. I was not used to getting severely sweated by a babe.

She awoke rubbing her hands across the ab-jured[20] area of her maternal swelling. She patted it a few times and smiled. I smiled back. Her hair frizzled over her shoulders, capturing the last and final rays of sun shining through the lodging curtains. A delicate cluster of strands were caught in the trail of saliva ac-cumulating at the corner of her mouth. She removed it and softly opined.

"I hope that we have a happy family. Where have you been?"

"Outside of your dreams."

"No, for true."

A wild scent escaped from her wanton pores. It tasted in the middle of sweat and sex. I returned.

"Outside, walking. I watched the Goldfinch's sing in the wind and stuck myself with a napkin." I paused, "in the nose to kill some boogers."

"She laughed histrionically, suddenly stopping, making reference with both her eyes and pointing fin-gers, to an abrupt movement in her abdominal cavity. We both held careful eyes of examination with our combined senses and curbed humors.

"I was out thinking. You know, I have serious problems with Ed Meese as Attorney General. He's not even a lawyer. He probably didn't pass the bar. But then again, maybe, he took it in Pennsylvania."

"Where did you pick that from?"

I can't recall where but it was a legitimate source."

"Well...," she paused.

"A mammal."

"Honestly,...the president has the executive right to appoint the Attorney General."

"That should show you how fucked up shit is over here. I mean you would not understand, they

---

[20] Retracted.

72

look at you as a foreigner. You look at yourself as a foreigner. I was walking outside. I played with a few caterpillars. And they reminded me of when me and some of my friends would be shooting craps. We were all school boys, and me and my boy the only real hard niggers there. We had big pots. Three, four hundred "da-la's."

"You'd be surprised of what would come out of them nights. That's where I think I heard that shit about Ed Meese."

"You miss your friends?"

"Na. Them mother fuckers don't do nothing but keep me in trouble. But they do give me a lot of strange shit to write about."

"You miss them, oui?"

"We." I had not thought that I missed them just that I had decreased in the production of letters by two fold.

No short stories. A few contemplations of titles for novels, plays and the sort. Just roughly a dozen poems. I do not think that she could comprehend the feeling. To me, it was just like impotency. But I was not impotent and realized that if me and my boy Trojan were still a tag team and remained active, we would never suffer brain drain.

She comforted me then as she had done so many times before. And there was music again, that of the Northern Oriole and the Goldfinch and the ever-present Catbird.

By now, dreaming and I were real close. Like me and Black Magic, and Fontain, and Tony, and Willie and Leon. And the noble birds that orchestrated the wondrous and sovereign secrets of sound that no record or laser disk could ever reveal without the assistance of humid, dry air.

We flowed smoothly together into the rich fields of make-believe. I was with my boys. Let's see, Tony, Leon, Fontain and Black Magic. There was a huge 24 inch colored cathode ray tube. Not a computer, however. Tony was next to a giant speaker on a skateboard. Both Fontain and Leon were holding their dicks and Willie was on the phone. The tray was passed to me. Thus the conversation begins. I hung up the phone.

"Who was that?" Tony asked, flipping in shit."

"Willie."

"He coming' over or what?

"Or what!" Leon exclaimed.

"Man, they sweating' jones hard up in her'", Fontain commented."

"Who?" I asked.

"The music group?" Black Magic questioned.

"Ollie North, stupid jones." Fontain closed.

"Ah, contra - Iran jones. Aaa." I understood.

"Aaa", several of them replied at the same time.

"He's a tight boy kind of. I like the way in particular how he whispers, every now and then, with his lawyer." Tony added.

"But we all know that if jones was a nigger, he'd be getting the book and library thrown at him. They got mother fuckers thinking that jones is a hero." Leon opined putting out his cigar.

"Jones gone end up jus' like Erlichman. Nixon jones." I added.

"And what happen to black jones who told on everybody? Can't get a job nowhere. Jones right there gone get taken care of. He taking the blame for his boys." Black threw out, accenting every phrase with a head motion.

The scenario altered for a moment. The feeling was as if I had pulled a phone number from my billfold void of name and could not recall of the subject whom had awarded it to me. The music was created by Until December - *Slave*.

A grey and distressingly magnetic suggestion was offered by Tony. I could tell that it was fueled by tremendous emotional indifferences.

"Let's make a movie", he said. "We all got credit cards, I'll go and get the books tomorrow."

Smiles and laughs contaminated the room indicative of serious contention. We had all wanted to be something other than what we were, I do believe. We were artist at heart and provocative by nature. Tony use to tell me of how he wanted to be able to walk up in clubs and sit at a piano and play some Milt Jackson, and mack all the hoes. But football lead him astray.

Both Black and Fontain were actors and indigenous comedians by trade. Fontain always stated how "they would never ever give a mother fucker like him a show like David Letterman's". While Black wanted to be on the other station, standing as the prosecuting attorney counter posed to Perry Mason, never failing to defeat I might add.

Leon wanted no parts of any of the previous. He just wished simply to retain his fame as an international playboy. He would be content working old women in support of our activities.

But in order for it to manifest, they would need a writer. A computer was situated in the corner on an end table. I headed towards it. I sat down, but companioned with mutilated wrist.

I produced nothing.

CHAPTER 8
CASTRATION

Dreaming.

Dreaming.

Dreaming, dreaming, dreaming.

Dreaming. That's the way I feel when I'm just with myself, alone with thought. Not even the stupid things that others consider to be important matter to me. Maybe it is because before I always get to anything, stable, acceptable, contra-to science, I walk through what ya might call mental gardens. Past E. Franklin Frazier, Moranda Smith, Daniel Hale, Thomas Szaszs, Diop, Hemmingway and sorts of that type. Listening, occasionally questioning, debating or downright refuting what they believe, or maybe even reading one of their unpublished dictates, when it applies, and regarding it more important than any projective test, grade, semester report, bill, law or any genre applied. That's what's up here. That's me. Wrong or right, who gives a fuck. It never made a difference when I was drinking my own blood; politically, economically and/or culturally.

I actually knew, for certain, for a fact, that I was schizophrenic. So to the point that fear did not attempt to crawl into the fluid corpus of my life, or jump through the flooded caverns of my sometimes, seemingly plastic mind.

I had discovered, by complete accident one day that by making Margarita mad, the urge to write spawned through me. Through my hands and feet and arms and legs. Not to mention my brain. It started at the park.

We were walking through the woods, the seeds of the Aspen's glittered the lake like snow. Birds sang and the blue of the sky was such that it appeared invisible. The battered and antiquated trail that we plodded was more than an adventurous escapade for Nicole.

She was 18 months at the time. She was remarkable and only thoughts of spoiling her feasted through my mind.

After she was born, we moved back to the city. Margarita wanted her to be exposed to the more avaricious and glamorous settings in life. I wanted her to be able to chop wood, play chess, read, write, do calculus, and cook.

That night we were scheduled to attend a party at one of her girlfriends house. Nicole would spend the evening with Jimmi and we would go out as planned.

At the party, we danced and enjoyed ourselves to the extent to which the circumstances would permit. With my indifference however, through pragmatism and reason, I concluded that the limits that I had contemplated concerning the evening, were meant for everybody else. The women made me wonder of the rainbow, of the NBC peacock when it was in full swing. It seemed as if each color was representative of a particular hair style.

The music was mild, heartwarming. Muted cornets and the likes. That was, until the DJ got to popping. The curtains, a copper blue and the food, without hot sauce. I was patient.

I noticed in the corner, near this glowing vase of ferns, dried ferns, the kind you buy in the fake plant section of a major department store, Tiana.

Tiana used to be crazy about me -- so she said. Until she experiences some new rebirth. We were friends and firmly believed that we would be forever.

I wonder what is it about me that leans to describing the legs first, of every woman that I visually receive. Realism, I guess that I know what I am all about. Besides, it's better than thinking of them as a computer, wouldn't you say?

They were stilts enameled in sable, standing proudly against the wall. They were fuming gases of softness, floating through the air with the greatest of ease. There personified structure was as if the woman, on the flying trapeze.

Until that instance, life had seemed, with the exception of Nicole, an entire contradiction. I thought this but I lived that. I wanted this but I had that. It perturbed me to the point sometimes that I wondered about the wisdom that I had often proclaimed to represent. Was I wise and brilliant for real? Or was I just another crazy mother fucker who knew that where he was, and how he wanted to make it, depended solely on the fruit of mother nature and reason. Yes, a contradiction. I will die knowing that I will have represented the unquestionable task of being as nothing but a contradiction. A dichotomy among all paradigms of existences.

But it made me happy. The contradiction had deserted me. And it was personal instability that made me want to write, and record the shit that I relegated as pertinent in my life in the first place. Tiana had reminded me of that turmoil and conflict -- those things that created the urge to admire beauty and laugh at it all. Without the principle of contradiction, I would just go around with nothing to prove, with no one to refute me or what I perceive to be real. No more challenges and no more triumphs. I would probably miss victory most of all. But Tiana contradicted everything that exaggerated that evening.

I had never been able to control my body to the fullest. Mother nature had rendered me almost completely harmless, allowing me the honor of being able to use eight percent of my brain. I was lucky, most denizens operated at about the level of three percent. Need I not remind you that the unit of measure employed is the life span of a human organism.

Anyway, Margarita was somewhere about the area chatting with the host and several mutual friends. I had already eaten more than a dozen raw oysters and two times that many celery sticks dipped in this shit mixed with mayo. I was just about to complete my third strawberry daiquiri, and visions of a fourth had accumulated uproariously in concernment to the thought. Everyone knew Margarita but not too much of me. It was fun, I must admit, stuffing my face while at the same time, trying not to explode with too much dignity. But it seemed to just slip out. But that is what a respectable up-bringing will get you.

The D.J. had been juking for a while and moving my head appeared to be my sole response. I had not danced with anyone. One lady asked me to dance but I was eating and drinking and being festive at the time. Instead, I approached Tiana.

She informed me that she had just taken a job at this female counseling center. She was the Coordinating Counselor and her duties, among other things, entailed the distribution of condoms. She recommend that I stop by one day and pick some up. She even said that I could get up to six dozen if I asked for her. She also informed me that Leon and Tony were staying in my crib. From what she said, they knew that I was with Margarita, of that I was now a father and that I had something to do with a missing Dice agent.

I was stunned and almost grinned when she asked if I had killed him. I igged her respectfully and directed the conversation from there on out.

We started talking about the old days, You know, the times we use to bone at regular intervals. I'm sure you are somewhat familiar with coming up on a person whom, at one point of time you were ecstatic about, and immediately want to jump in the sack with, just for old times' sake. She was fine, not to subtract nothing away from Margarita's last name. But I could see in her, the rational, the reason, the nature behind the concept of why I had selected her sustenance to conquer in the first place. She was ravishing and her legs were like some new and dramatic piece of software -- tempting.

Of course, I propositioned her for the panties, and she responded the negative in an instance.

Quickly, I re-worded my injuring questions.

"Do you remember", I questioned. "Of the past. Not like it is important now, but do you?"

She looked up with both eyes, moving away from that container of artificial ferns, removing her lips from the straw that was frozen in between her ginned-out refreshment, and nodded her head in the affirmative.

"Was that sign language?" I asked, contemplating whether or not I should go back over to the table and eat some more of that tuna fish type stuff. But I waited, and resumed my line of questioning.

"You can talk to me at least, can't you? It's just another party."

She pointed to the DJ's booth and remarked, "I came with him."

I looked, at first, in disbelief, and suddenly started to smile.

"He's jamming", I opined. "Jones seems to be a pretty cool to me."

She motioned her cranial cavity in agreement. I decided to go back to the table, but this time to grab a handful of chicken wings. I returned. she asked for one. I thought to my lonesome for a moment, just like consultation I guess, to plan my next strategic move.

I picked the largest leg, or wing, or whatever, up, and aimed it in the direction of her oral cavity. I gave her a little taste. Of course, she tried to bite of more than she could handle.

"It's hot", she stated, looking at it, and then at me and the puritanical simper that had formed pretentiously over my face.

"Blow on it," I returned.

She laughed and proceeded to take my advice.

"You like it," I continued, laughing on the inside as if I had been punished, and knew that I was correct.

An empty and swollen yes rolled from her tongue. And, it seemed, the wider she opened her mouth, the more I cherished my self-induced activity. It was as if I was allowed to play all day, on a day when it was scheduled for me to cut the grass. Then she caught on. The further she obtrude her carpet of taste into the intergalactic terrain of the atmosphere, the deeper I shoved those drummets. We did not stop until several bones were completely in the raw.

"You meat-eater," I said, rolling the last bone around her compendious[21] lips.

From her simper I could detect that her next response would be a growl, but that, in all accords, would be opposite of her formless, social manifesto.

"I'm glad to see that you have been doing well for yourself."

She swallowed what was in her mouth and remarked. "I will always excel in everything I do."

"Oh, so you're a Hyundai now, 'ey?"

Janet Jackson's, *The Pleasure Principle* was providing the background, with the notorious exception of laser lights penetrating about the area like some empty and balding wave of heat. On inadequate grounds, I contrived to get her to languish on her perspectives of the Murchison Meteorite and directed panaspermia. We moved outside, gazed into the seared wingspan of the quarter moon and discussed with passion, our appreciation for that exceptionally, fine brandy, Tequila. I was like a snake captured in the structure of a man, ready to bite her ankles, or whatever piece of flesh, was first revealed to me.

She always said that I was blind with molten talent, and that the world was mine to conquer. Margarita had never told me such things, and it was my fault, because I never told her, or spoke to her about my writing as I did with my casual and impermanent associates.

She honored me on my dress again and started to take the lead in retrospect. She asked what had I been up to, what had I been doing with my life. I lied, I told her that I was completely happy and that Margarita had purchased for me, a new computer. The unau-

---

[21] Concise.

thentic stillness of the star-glittered, blanket of a sky seemed louder to me, than the music.

And when that special beat came around, every now and then, she would take hold of her petite French lace skirt, keeping motion with that simple gregarious and shiny wave of notes, smiling, and taunting me as if she had just snatched all my marbles, like she was playing for keeps and I was playing for funs. Her appearance was exhibited in a fashion that would accelerate both night and day.

Her lips moved again. "You miss the old times, don't you?"

With my left hand firmly hidden in the outer coat pocket of my chalk-stripe, wool suit and my head surfing on that same wave, I blurted "I guess so. I thought this was a party."

Still flaunting her measured autumn complexion against the radiance of the moon she replied, "Well, I guess that they got neighbors."

"That shouldn't make a difference. You know the ones we used to throw. Crap games in the basement, or the kitchen, everybody taking turns mixing it up, and the smell, the taste of cheeba floating around the joint. And don't mention joint. And all the hoes, I mean babes would be there."

"Remember when Tony would go out of town, and how whenever Ron Reagan did something fucked up, he'd call me, or I'd call him -- which meant that our phone bills were astronomical...."

I would have continued but, I think it was the way in which she brushed her breast against my arm. When she reached for the folded pocket square squinting out and away from my lapel that interrupted one of my exciting and almost usually expanded oral expositions. I don't think that she was offended by me using the work "ho" in its plural form. She knows that I tend not to notice whether or not my cynical remarks upset others. After all, I had her to thank for this reformation I considered myself to be going through.

She removed from her clutch, the envelope of what I gathered once held her invitation. She wrote her phone number on it with her lipstick, something that I had seen only in old detective and THINMAN movies. She did not ask me for a pen so I knew that her actions were premeditated. Planned. She folded the envelope in to a portable little square and placed it into the auspices of my handkerchief and returned it to its original position. She kissed my hand and entered back into that orchard of fungi and nihilistic annoyance.

I myself, waited outside a while, didn't want to give old girl nothing to trip on. I had managed to get a comic book from one of the kids wandering about the party. They were sent to bed at eleven thirty.

I cherished the reading material in a verminous and splendid manner -- The X-Men, even laugh and saying "oh Boy", out loud and to myself. After all, I was just my Momma's baby.

Margarita was looking ever so marvelous and, I could detect that she knew what she was doing to the immediate parameter of the male population collected at the time. She adored it, and all of the attention it gave her glowing ego. I even feed it a morsel or two every now and then. I had already gone up to her a few times, when she was addressing some other associates, and say, "that's a fat ass rock you totin' there lady". She'd just laugh it off and continue on with whatever she was into at the time.

We danced too. Seven times in a row, when the cornets were soft and shit. I was kind of famished at the time and a mixture of exotic and country smells would not let me forget it.

By the time she had found me, I knew that she had been missing me, she was that type. The type that thought that going to the movies and eating was a date. She had no premonitions of the advantages of going down to the local market and tuning in to PBS.

She saw me sitting outside, by my lonesome, enjoying the parting privilege of a comic book. I did not buy it, they cost about seventy five cents now. Too much for a desperate and self-accepted man of letters to purchase.

First, off, she questioned its attainment. I told her the truth. Miraculously, she believed it. Eventually she got so perturbed that she started to whimper an demanded that we pick up Naja and return home. She did not speak to me for the duration of the night. Even when we were at home, safely sufficient in our bed and Naja next to our sides she turned her body a complete ninety degrees, and I suspect, looked at the red display of the radio alarm until she went to sleep.

CHAPTER 9
FERMINTATION

There in front of me sat a scotch tumbler filled half-way with a Cabernet-Blanc and a fresh cup of Sanka. It was decaffeinated and I was trying to stay awake. My grandmother had raised me on Sanka since the age of five. It was use what I was to. Just like I was use to cooling out peacefully with my computer and Steel Pulse.

It had gotten to the point where I concerned myself with much of nothing. Except for Nicole. I use to think that being a father was the greatest adventure thinkable. I was right, but being a common law husband was another color.

I still desired and longed for the artificial theology that Margarita and I had developed, and even felt as if everything between us represented some primitive religion of nature. Her sex was very much irreverent and sizzling, if I might interject. Being inside of her was like sipping on a thickly rummed Mai Tai. Proportioned well between her notorious and exceptional gammons, I would fall asleep, cradled like a baby.

Then there were her hands. They held in their compartment of touch unlike no other. Though she believed that she did not project a perfect shape, the spring fever that was evident between us was more than a cognition that brought forth awareness on tactile stimulation.

She was dialectical, making me always think the opposite thought. Thinking me away even from the supposition of putting imagination to paper.

Sometimes at night, we would prance about dimly, next to the heated glow of candles and music, with Nicole snorkeling pulls from her bottle as if it represented some ritual incantation of our swarthy and kryptonic past. Our motions were like those of flies, whom had become trapped inside for a few days, making their last salable plea to the surrounding doors and windows.

Two years had passed by and everything was just like yesterday.

I was sitting at the desk. I had just poured myself a glass of the double X amber Mexican brew. The forth bottle and a copy of *A Short History of the Ancient World* by Smith and Moorhead was in my view. I had just put it down. I had only read four chapters and it was disturbing to note that the only credit that they awarded to Hannibal, was that of being tagged as the aggressor, and loser in the second and third Punic Wars. The thought alone, made me sick to the stomach. I don't know if I will ever want to complete it. But I most likely will, uncompleted shit gets on my fucking nerves.

I had been with my tender bit a while. I cared for her and preoccupied myself with her safety. But that is why I did not want to spend my time with a lot of women. It seemed as if all of my time was some of their time. Before I was blending with Margarita, I was seriously considering to cool down a bit. It was getting to the point where I was associated with more women than stories I had to write.

Nicole's middle name was Naja, as in Naja Nigricollis. I had always wanted to name my seed as such. I would never tell Margarita that I truly concerned myself, to the fullest in reference to her well-being. I would never be able to tell her that I really wanted to be with her, and by her side forever, if such a thing existed. I would never tell her that writing was more important to me than her. I did not even think that the courage was within me to inform her of my cavorted preoccupations. At times, my situation appeared worse than having three children, two car notes and a mortgage. Seemed that the next day would prove to be another Gin drinking holiday. And I did not even like Gin. It was all that was around. Just like that history book I was speaking of.

The next morning, I was still in place, behind the same old ugly typewriter. The Blue and White of clear Corona bottles littered the lightly emotional atmosphere of the day. There was not much to do. I could not think of anything exceptional. I really did care for Margarita and Nicole. But things seemed to dictate a different tune, a different note.

The other day, for the purposes of changing the environment, we had sex in the car. I made the choice to put on a mask. And under the mask, my eyes were closed. She got upset, and I was able to write about it.

At first, It kind of upset me. Thinking of how much it must have hurt her, knowing, believing that I did not want to see her face when we had sex. But I did not consider the thought for too long. In fact, I rejoiced over the mere implications of such an action. I wrote and wrote and wrote. Not just titles to stories for future consideration, but of real and detailed events, as they took the time to cross and drag and stumble across my personal constructs and neural features.

My frustrated nature was only for the minute, I could always find patience and relief by holding Naja in my arms.

I took more time, being with her, holding her in my arms, reading to her, and telling her stories, that Margarita seemed to be of no true importance to me. It seemed as if my habits now, were like that of the frog's breath, brainstorming through the night, searching for fire and flies. If there was no fire, there was no inspiration and if there were no flies, or insects, there was starvation. I cherished Margarita for her integral part in the production, and every moment that I looked in Naja's face, I could envisage my past memories of pleasure that Margarita had shared with me. She would never know that my actions and heart were sincerely dedicated to her, and as I said before, she would never know. I had read of shit like this in books and had relegated all to be just mere rumors of a fictional heart. Maybe it was just cold outside.

Sometimes, I would not even speak. Not until she had given me the cue to jump down her throat. I would even try to make her cry, something that she appeared to do or manifest or produce whenever I questioned her. It was like a senate hearing. Her personal sustenance versus the laws and contingencies of reinforcement held in high esteem by all proponents of the pen.

But above all, it did not make me feel bad. On the contrary, it made me perceive myself as some sort of Hehe or Zulu warrior, on some type of quest, trying to find the opposite answer in the land of one answer. It was confusing but not enough to divert my instincts to that somber ground of the copyright. But so much for despondency.

I looked around the apartment, which Margarita had selected to represent her lingua Franca of interior decorating. Yellows, greys, and socially noxious hues of indigo surrounded me, rendering me immune to humor and optimism. I played a few cuts by the Bus Boys. First *Anggie*. It took a few minutes for me to recuperate, to catch my breath. A new tenderness arose in me by the time *D-Day* and *Tell The Coach* came on, dissolving my pseudo-inherent limitation.

After a few, abrupt intakes of air, I was good to go. I had no other choice. I had to dedicate my life to writing, as invaluable an activity as it was, or seemed to be accepted. No matter how much I knew she was to me, she would have to ride the bench. Naja would join writing, becoming the single chambers of my heart. So what if I had to make her mad. She would understand, eventually before she departed this world of the flesh. So what. I'd just have to dedicate a book to her.

She was gone shopping. So I decided to write about the time we were in the car, coming from the market. Naja had a cold and it had been raining for most of the afternoon. Everything was displayed as if emblematic of the promotion of continuous formlessness and the separate expression of consultation.

We discoursed eagerly, of her arcane initiatives and my rather obvious flaws.

I had left a Corona bottle in the middle of the floor. The way she opined, it was like a Hydrogen bomb that had destroyed thirty million folks.

I told her that I had left if there accidently and that I had been using it as a target for putting. When I told her that she was the one that insisted that I relax, and do shit like that in an effort to write more. She did not exactly say it like that, but that was what she meant at the time. I guess that she was feeling helpless for me, in an immensely delicate way, no doubt. Anyway, she was full of clamorous talk and expressed in so many words the fact that sometimes, she did not know if I was no better than an insect. She would chant:

> "Niggers and flies
> I do despise
> the more I see nigger's
> the more I like flies."

I think that it was the only direct quote she knew of. I started to jump down her throat verbally, but Nicole was strapped in the back seat, tripping off of the whole situation. She was not crying, but anybody could discern at the time, that her state would eventually accede to such. She appeared so metallic and clear. Just like a scarlet flower, revealing its first petals to the sun and its colleagues.

Instead, I turned towards the window and paid her no attention. Watching rain rippling creeks flow westward against the curb side and designing formations of sediments, beneath miniscule lakes of water, or oasis of weeds and grasses, flushing through the cracks of the black top, clenching my fist repetitively, not even listening to what she had to say, listening to some Steely Dan -- until she turned it off -- and counting the difference in seconds, between the lighting and the thunder. I looked at Naja again. She was donnish with tears.

I only produced eleven pages, and I was used to fourteen or fifteen. It was better than nothing and brought to my face, after re-reading it, a smile of fulgurous passion. It was indeed different operating without a computer, but no hardship was worth more than the feeling it gave me. I was still the shit, at least to my lonesome. And that's all who really counted once a nigger really looked at it. It just so happens that there are some things that a bro got to do to keep in communication with himself. I know that commitments are what's up. But it just so happens that I want as few as possible.

I was so involved in what I was doing, that I burned up a few grilled cheese sandwiches. No problemo. Just scrape them off and eat them anyway. So involved that I forgot about the album. So I changed it. *Cosmic Slop* was next in line for the wheels of steel.

I started writing again. This time, however, it was an essay. I was happy, and at the same instance, mad as shit. I had read in some newsletter of economics, that this guy that I held in high esteem -- when it came to thinking about capital --, with the initials J.K.G., had raised, as an issue of planetary importance, concerning the future of these United States of America. He stated that the incessant new highs of the stock market would eventually result in the toppling of this system current scheme of money-making and capital formation and would resemble the flat-out boom of 1929. I was mad not because this individual was right or nearer to my visions of Panglossonomics, but because I had thought of the same shit and talked about the same fate with my friends more than a year ago. So in order to release my steam, I decided to write what was on my mind, down that instant, to avoid future embarrassment. Who knows, maybe he had read my article in that scrawny newsletter I used to submit my moderate opinions to. But I doubt it.

The apartment still smelled of burnt bread when I heard the chambers of the dead-bolt turn. Margarita entered with what appeared to be several thousand bags of merchandise. I placed the first short story in my briefcase and, in a rather prescient manner, resumed my "see-no-evil" activities. Naja ran to me mumbling and saying several new words that I had never heard her utter prior. "Charge me one of that." She said with a exacting sound, pointing to the putter perched superciliously against the wall.

"Go and get your ba-ba for mommy." Her accent was like a pasha in a harem of words sponsored by a cheap French/ English dictionary. I would never be able to remove the shuddered profile, or the requisite figure that amorously seared my erotic being.

Naja ran into the kitchen, with her feet heavy with dalliance, full-throttle, reaching to sedate her raging appetite for her liquid refreshment. She returned, running into my arms. And I held her firmness next to mine as if it were a rose, or my first grade report, free of unsatisfactory and marks other than those representing excellence. She kissed me hard, all over my face, telling me, in her exact words, "Naja missed daddy". And in the same montage of affection, showing me her new yellow, high-top Converse.

Margarita took her from me and proceeded to prepare to give her a bath. Several clear, sharp and desperate "no's" exited her mouth. She started to cry. I told her to be a big girl and that I would tell her a story. I don't know why I told her to act as something she was not, but it was the first thing that came from my parted lips. She smiled and went about her way.

Latter on that night, Margarita questioned me about the burnt smell about the house. I was listening but, to be truthful and honest, I had other thoughts on my mind. Thoughts that were subtracted of material derision and full of febrile waves of impending physical confrontation. She was succinctly venting her displeasure. I told her that it was an accident and that I was writing at the time when it happened. She paid my remarks, little or no attention. I tried to explain. I do not know if it was because of my visible erection, or due to the fact that I as used to explaining my developmental actions, as I did when anything suddenly entered my presence in the form of a problem. Women had proven to be difficult to maintain and handle, although rather easy to get. And still, I did not see what they saw in me, and ten times out of ten, we were using the same mirror. I wanted her so much.

"I leave you here and you destroy everything that we have worked for, as a family", she stated without guile and pettiness.

"I cleaned up the mess and burned a few incense too."

"Don't get smart with me. You just bug me, it seems, most of the time now. I don't know why I didn't stay with Robert."

"De-con's in the cabinet."

She began to sob. I brought her close to me. Her hands, firmly tightened in my grasp. She avoided me, unsuccessfully, when I started to kiss, and nibble, and taste her disingenuous hate. She continued to resist. I paid no attention.

I just rather, at the time, linked it with some type of business mentality, the kind that was frequent to spurt-out unctuous lies; anything to sway the buyer. Margarita knew that I was beyond such random pettiness. She knew that the animal in me would seek salvation in the inchoate junctures of her flesh.

For a minute it seemed like a stormy day in New York -- as yellow and black as bumble bees. Taxis and asphalt and rain and people. I was a real person, or at least I considered myself to be. I knew that there existed out there in the world, accordant to my empirical atmosphere, peoples and stuff that were not about playing games -- none other than those of respect and honor and patience, that is. And I was one of them. I thought her to represent the previous.

The bed was not available at the time, the table would have to do. The little Paul Lawrence Dunbar, skeleton-type typewriter contained its position sternly. A little while ago, I called this little piece of cherry a desk.

Then suddenly, my dreaming natured erupted. As I pressed my tongue deeply past her neck line, I thought of how she spoke of Robert, and how she wanted to be with him, and how I had not been writing like I used to, and how I cherished Naja, and how I wanted to take her body beneath me and smother it with fermenting passion and magical allurement.

I grabbed her flowing locks with my fist pulling her head back against the cherry wood surface. I pulled in a way not to hurt her, but to force her into my ways -- it was not difficult. She greeted my fury, pushing my fist, forcing more pain through her synapses. And that dress, I adored that dress, that hound's-tooth-checked tank dress with the zippered front. I thought of Naja again.

I could not remember the exact second or minute or hour, since time was considered a commodity to many, at which that blessed escapade of procreation occurred. I pretended to remake the entire operation as it would have been produced and directed by me, yours truly. She started with her zipper, I had other initiatives in mind. We met half way, down by the Rio Grande. The zipper halted at breast level and her skirt, near her waist. I believed the panties were tossed or burned or flung somewhere into the body-hugging reaches of the stainless universe.

Take it from a professional, there is nothing, no feeling, no language, no phrase, no punctuation mark no computer or no foreign beer like it. Maybe a few smorgasbords and some lighted tennis and basketball facilities, but not too much that could make a person -- genderless -- more, 'ey, rested. Rested. Relaxed.

I was not dreaming now. I had not paid any attention to the music. I should have known. *Frankie's First Affair* by Sade, her favorite and tops on my list also. All outside of the window held the attention of my eyes like I was a little boy playing with an ant nest. For a moment only. I thought of Naja again and helped her mother come to a mutual agreement.

CHAPTER 10
SUBTRACTION

Even through the pastel blue of my tinted glasses, the city displayed itself, foolishly attired in an inclement grey. It seemed just humid enough not to spawn a shower, but poky enough to keep newspaper boys and elderly outcast on the corners, selling, and digging for recyclable cans, spitting in the street as the cars stream past.

I was not of high station at the moment. I had been up all night tending to Naja. A stomach virus, fever or something in the area had taken over her. Her tears flowed until they flowed no more, depositing sedimentary films of saline atop her cheeks, still ever so rusty and brass. She had worn Margarita out completely.

I could only sit by her side, watching her sleep, something that she had not done all day. I could not get over the prescribed fact that she was mine, that my seed made her, or contributed to what she was. I could only sit there, even making myself think of the day she was born. The day before, I had been terribly ill, sick.

Although Brazil is well-respected for its crescent-shaped beaches and exotic vegetation. For some, it may even bring to dance the mixture of west coast traffic and samba rhythms mingling between the horns of the avenues, the Copacabana Beach or the Corcovado mountains. Whatever the case may be, when I think of Brazil and my luscious instructor -- *Teach Me Tonight*, thanks Al, I think of three things; the Club de Samba, that heartless song (*The Girl from Ipanema*) and Feijoada. A hot little dish comprised of black beans, smoked fish and sometimes, peas. And believe me, you, Margarita knows the way to my stomach, I mean, heart. I liked it just as much as I did her Moqueca, another little dish made of fish, shrimp, tomatoes and

97

peppers. I speak of this in such a way because I had been eating Feijoada all day. It was Margarita's fault I think that it had been in the ice box for about a month. But she was in mourning, or in labor or on her period or whatever they called it when a babe curses a mother fucker out all day and night just because the baby was kicking and I was the one who had "put her in the situation." She even cursed a nigger because she was in fear of her life, which through some teleological manner, was related to the fact that she weighed more than she had ever expected, not giving the pregnancy any credit. I had asked her if anything was in the kitchen and she poured a verbose collection of hot grits on my back. That was the last time I was at a hospital. Not for the oral whiplash -- lip lash-- that I received.

I was back in the hospital. Margarita and hospitals are, how do you say, insoluble -- so am I as you probably have already gathered. The harder events, circumstances and situations made themselves to be, the more refined and devastatingly resplendent she was to me. Everybody told me, all of her friends and Jimmi in particular, that she would shout and direct obscene words at me. She did not. Instead, she called for me, reaching for the callous tenderness of my hand. She held tight.

I only wanted everything to be straight.

If only her fever would go down, I thought, then everything would be cool.

I just laid there. My pedantic dreaming had gone through a cease fire, for a while at least.

I'm glad that it was raining and shit. If we had to suffer, Margarita and Naja and me, then let it rain on the entire mother fucking world.

Between the large diaphanous surface of the window and the operatic-like background of the room, and the limpid shadows of chairs and portable cots, I expanded and revealed my eyes to the pinched and frightened, amnesia-causing, tabloid fanaticism that had transformed and ordered so much of my life. Just the Sun-Times this time.

I read page after page after page after page. It engendered a sense of curiosity, as if I had picked it up out of sheer boredom. Like reading Shakespeare when you really, truly, deep-down in your structure believed that actually, you were reading the works of Francis Bacon. Low-voltage shit, almost like it was the single remaining cloister of a vivified preliterate society. It was too responsible to fascinate me, not glitzy enough. Past tense now. But the window, the rain, the snot-like congested city walkways below me and the gravid appearance of buildings, flattened out in relief form, against the ubiquitous hemlines of telephone poles, took me away from the loopy, state of distraction supplied by the hospital.

It had proved stronger, in many respects, stronger than even the state of dreaming, but only for a second.

I don't need to remind you that this was merely temporary.

Spock. Spock.

This babe once, sent me a post card in the mail, with Spock on it. Black and white. Funny, ain't it. Back to my mild solace or insight. The score with Spock was like; emotions and stupidity 0? mackness and brilliance 2000 -- percent that is (can you end a sentence with a linking verb? Well, I guess you can.)

Spock seemed to float through the window. Four quarts and a phaser was all that was with him. Bull. Everything in the hospital was at a standstill, even the denizens below me were at a halt. A mellow prattle from the bottles came into the room as if they were held in a metal test tube rack.

He sat the brew down and went for the radio. For some reason or another, a large, five piece Akai audio system held firmly against the wall outlined against the voiceless oak influences of a pair of Boise speakers. They seemed to influence or alleviate all the pain, all the mystic temperament that a life of constant dissipation could proffer.

Spock was familiar with the equipment. The manner in which he adjusted the devices, hinted to a gross organizational fetish on his behalf. I pardoned him and just figured that it was a fluent and natural manifestation of his meticulous array of reinforcement contingencies. What used to be an unattractive atmosphere, an environment of unspoiled beauty and trudged-out, unauthentic comfort, was now, introduced in absentia to the reposing stillness of Robert Cray's *Strong Persuader*.

"She was right next door, and I'm such a strong persuader, she was just another notch on my guitar...."

In a barely audible rumble an without illusion, he said. "You know that you do not belong on earth. In the sense that the concept of gravity presents unlimited immunity. You should be Poet Laureate of the universe and dark matter. Of time and infinity of reason and enlightenment. That should be a piece of plutonium after you clip your nose hairs."

I knew that with the access to such a unit of complete stratification, there had to exist a higher level, a pinnacle, humor.

I responded, "I guess that your point is valid, given the fact that my government is totally alienating itself from the public and the rest of the world. Agoraphobic, you know. And you know me Spocky baby, I got to at least get to prove my point. Given infinity and the propagation of photons, do you think that my ability to capture, control, record and satirize events, functions and certain mental contemplations, that I deem as an oft-heard and a diminished sort of art, and most importantly, humor, will ever give me enough stimulation to privilege such a position?"

"Most definitely, you can hold your dick with both hands, can you not?"

I smiled and he passed me a brew.

"Got to get going. Vulcan women, I tell you the truth. Butta, Black, you got a joint for the road?"

I don't know where the quarter came from, but I gave it to him. He smiled again and left me with a quote.

> "Only we, we emancipated spirits, possess the prerequisite for understanding something nineteen centuries have misunderstood..."

I think it was Nietzsche. I can't really place it, but I'm almost sure. The only Nietzsche that I had enjoyed the liberties to conquer, to understand, were volumes of his works that comprised his life span written in German. For some reason or another, I considered that the English versions would lack in actual content and meaning. German, strange, I could read it but not speak it. Then too, it was the *Year of the Cat*, the way Al Stewart and the radio signal put it.

Grey again, was the hospital. Blue was the music. Passionate and magnetically above the level of any social facade.

Margarita had awaken, done in a manner in which the commoner would consider to be an action exemplarily of an expensive price tag. The only thing that I recalled of the paper, was that the Dusky Sea Side Sparrow had become extinct. That another one of my cohorts on the endangered species list was gone. Would I be next?

Supporting herself on her arms, stretched with her back perpendicular to the wall, she yawned and spoke.

"Have you had any sleep?"

Her voice, verminous and splendid and fresh and delectable -- like melons.

"A little, but never enough, you know."

She glowed with security. What was once a beer handed to me by a certain science officer, was now a Styrofoam cup of "industrial-strength coffee".

The way in which she said special words. The "no" that meant confirmation, the "what", which seemed to always come when she answered the phone any four letter word or brief phrase, had an immense influence on me.

Her eyes scanned the traversed and darkly corrupted structures in the cell. Just for a space, she was without the non-personal forces of reflective self-conscious, exhibiting a locution that closely defined fright, or fear.

"Come here", she whispered with her middle finger.

She held me in a manner that drew a reciprocated reaction from me. And she felt good too. A very warm feeling it was, fueled by enough emotional indifference to ask, "What's she doing?"

"Sleeping Well", I returned. With my lips within a tongues distant from hers.

In her arms was where I remained. A slippery rustle of blue hospital air breezed towards us when the door opened. The elderly white gentleman, somewhere in the vicinity of fifty, seemed to situate himself in a manner in which his belt could best support his stomach, leaning on the nightstand as if he was waiting for a call-out order for some chicken wings at a Chinese stop and cop.

His hair, white. His smock, white. his teeth, white. his humor invisible.

"How yall today? I tell ya, they got everything from chicken nuggets chicken squares, chicken strips and wherever you get them, one still has to remind them to add sauce. I guess that it helps cut overhead. Cheap, but wise. Hump...." He commented, scratching his belly and rubbing his forehead at the same time. Something that I could not do until the fourth grade.

Probably due to a dilapidated substania nigra or ineffective substation of a certain catecholamine -- on his behalf of course.

He continued to relax himself, which entailed a great deal of talking about nothing. I even did it myself sometimes. About once every two or three leap years.

I in turn, moved about the room blankly, taking up in this geometrically designed, cubical of a chair. Metal and leather mainly. Dr. Bruce tilted his bifocals over that bridge of a nose of his and began scanning, I should hope, reading, the Aluminum encased chart.

"Naja Nicole." He read out loud.

"What have your test concluded." Margarita asked, sitting up on the edge of the cot as she fought a drifty battle; trying to prevent clusters of strains of hair from blowing into the side of her mouth. Finally getting to the point where she pulled an elastic band from her powdery wrist, holding it with her mouth like some tenuous creature of erotic bewilderment stretching and brushing and teasing and shaking her ink black locks into one pony tail.

He spoke in tone somewhere in the middle of astonishment and certainty. "It seems that Naja is extremely responsive to formic acid."

"What, we do not keep any acids around the house." Margarita exploded, running over instantly, to check on her baby.

In interrupted. "Formic acid is commonly found in the stinging chemical released by ants, bees, and hornets when they sting."

"Very well put Mr. Love. I must add that in this particular case, the culprit was a wasp. Scliphron cementarium." He added with a detailed thumping of his pen against the chart.

I threw in. "In females, the ovipositior serves as the stinging apparatus."

"Why didn't they tell us this the other times we've taken her to the doctor?"

"Well," he returned. "They don't normally run test to detect if a person is allergic to formic acid or things like vinegar. Do not get me wrong, such things are possible."

Margarita, bemoaned by the mere idea of negligence, appeared to retract, briefly, into the brooding landscape of tissue paper and metal bed railings. She contorted her face grotesquely, attempting, I presuppose, to remain undimmed by the doctor's commentary. An efficacy of a more strident feint, no doubt.

Dr. Bruce, with that ladder of a neck of his, seemed to look like one of the figures or shapes of textures that I had associated to my penis, in one of its states. In fact, if it were not for the hair, he could have passed for a large, uncircumcised dick -- bipedal, standing up right, but not hard or erect. The only other way I could describe him was to mention the name Hans Kanters.

"You can take Naja home", he said in a wintry tone. "Just make sure she receives her medication four times a day. Bring her back in one week. We just want to make certain." He positioned himself over her dormant structure and smiled. A gracious smile. Warm and filled to the brim with sincere intentions and puritanical optimism.

As the long-simmering growls of my stomach concluded and the colorless, midnight darkness approached, I started to worry again. Think that maybe things would be alright, and simultaneously, that they would not. Thinking about Trotsky: "Without a contiguous lineage, and consequently, without a tradition, there cannot be stable progress."

The only questions I have are, what is stable and what is considered to represent progress?

Margie and Naja were asleep, dreaming together. I always wanted to know if silence was a sound. One can here silence. That is how it was at the moment. No more hospitals ringing of cute little beeps and page calls for doctors, who were probably somewhere freaking fresh, pert, first year nurses in empty rooms on the upper levels.

I left all of those thoughts behind when the central air popped on with its normally strident nobility. From there, you guessed it, I picked up a pad and started to jot down a few things. I was not working with that mother fucking, ass instrument many refer to as the type-writer any more. I would just have to leave it for the abhorrent immaturity that some wimp mother fuckers display when under the dominance of a close encounter of the last kind -- the computer; alas in wimp (weak interactive massive particles) terminology as a word processor.

I used to respect people like Mordecai Richler, traditionalist and the lot -- not completely. But, If he and he fellow solons would prefer to peck with two fingers on the greasy and rutted keys of a SMITH -- wonder if they are related to the beer people -- CORONA then go ahead. All that I can add is that productivity is what it is all about, storage is what it is all about, distribution is what it is all about. I have to go about writing seriously, taking each clamorous step, each sensitive corner, each deliberate back-spacing of the cursor and each web of rejection letters, just as serious as I would if I were talking a fine and intoxicating ornate of a woman out of her panties and into my bed.

As I stated earlier, I started to practice. I picked up this Vogue and this Playboy. Flipped through the pages. Umph. Nodding every now and then, in support.

Some pictures were noxious enough to elicit a response from that tag team of brain and pen. I wasn't getting off but practice makes perfect -- and I do not consider perfection to be attainable not even in the moment. Like I said at first, only wimps segment time to prove their points. But, I gonna show you what I got out of a few magazines.

TAKE 1: Claiming her hair with both hands, the gentle presence of tepid and poised armpits, hairless as they were, carried the rarity of a thousand moons, unctuously flowing across the fissures of her body. Curving under, and beneath her penchant breast. Shining just below her golden round nipples, pert, sparkling and erect. And still, there remained more curves and angles and too few colors left to describe her neurotic attraction.

TAKE 2: Examining the entire setting a little closer, taking it from the top down that is, she was holding steady at about ten feet. Outlined against the suede-like, Japanese-styled wall paper. The embroidered gold stripes shows exceptional taste, I suppose. Even If they don't, those fantastically culpable breast did.

TAKE 3: Her voice was like that of the harp. Breezy, flirty and enchantingly melodic. Like a nursery rhyme she was, of flesh and music. I had always pictured her the sort to entertain the cello. Playing it, strumming it, stroking its maple sides as if her sole paramour. Nudely draping her structure, with legs folded, in the middle of sonata and dance. Fred and Ginger like, in that grizzly brown backdrop, felt-like. Brown enough to complement the rosy fall color of the instrument. Lemony notes caress her nipples, they stand taller as it is peeled. The sonata is over, planned just for me.

So much for dreaming through the mediums of ink and pen.

Tennessee Williams and his medium Tom know what the deal is. It's like we both read Jacques Maritain.

> "There is nothing man desires more than a heroic life: there is nothing less common to men than heroism".

Tom would understand that life ain't much of shit without adventure. Anybody can look at a picture and put it to words in a few seconds -- sentences. But the real mack daddy was the one that lived adventure night and day, back to back and wrote that shit down on paper, in a certain way, and did not give a fuck if people hated it, but more so with personal satisfaction. That's what's up.

According to Tom, "Man by instinct is a lover, a hunter, a fighter and none of those instincts are given much play at (a warehouse). See what I'm saying?

> "........People go to the movies instead of moving. Hollywood characters are supposed to have all the adventures for everybody in America, while everybody in America sits in a dark room and watches them have them....." Tom

I left the magazines in place on the table, chewing on the pen as I cut off the light.

"Quelle horreur !!!"

I jumped when I heard the screaming. I didn't listen. I heard her call her desperately. "Naja". It was a dream. A loud dream. But I was not asleep.

Running into the bedroom with my eyes closed, I tripped over my own feet. It was a dream in real life. Why me?

CHAPTER 11
VISION

After the burial, there wasn't much for me to do, other than walk a lot. I did not need the exercise, but I did seem to feel somewhat better after the crisp and flattened moisture of a clear early October breeze smacked me in the face.

Just three days ago it was, the pomp and circumstance of ritualistic absurdity. I can see with every stroll of my limbs, the same brown Bermuda sod. It perturbed me severely, looking down at all that concrete, all them lines and at all those metal root protectors, thinking as I looked down at my shoes. Maybe because it was all I really paid attention to at the ceremony was the ground, watching my wing-tips sink dismally into the mud. It seems that all you do at funerals is listen and look down. I have never been one for looking down and yet I was doing it again. My grandmother had instructed me that it was improper conduct and a sign of impending weakness and self-hatred for a man to walk around with his head down.

I thought next of her, Margarita. Of how I did not want to speak to her. Not because she was inside reserving her temporal nature in a bubble bath, but just because I did not want too. I could face her but I did not want too. I did not want too. We had allowed ourselves, for four years, to enjoy and treasure the best that each could offer. The best consisting mostly of compassion, respect and sex.

She had provided me with a wish come true, a daughter. Nothing in my world had never touched that in me, or brought to the fore the same amount of needles emotion. Such that, as you can see led me on a quest ending at quantifying emotion as needless. Except, maybe for writing. Writing, as strange as it was, appeared as ancient as the art of war and more powerful than the dream. It was an intangible expression of self-reflection and meant more to me than any human ever would, ever did, ever could. My world was left and right.

There was no major conundrum for me to deal with. Just as the ivy grew on the brick buildings, so would writing, as I allowed it to take over my world. I was hoping like shit that it would manage my world. Make it something more than it appeared to the eye.

Before I could pause effectively at the red light confronting me, I found myself turning around in my tracks. I headed back to that glass of an apartment as condensation parted from my weathered lungs. I was no longer occupied with the impending legislation of thinking about death. I finally realized that I was already dead, just as dead as Naja. I could not explain it. It was just like the leaves; in the autumn when they brazed the world in opulent colors. The mystical patterns of bronze, gold, red, peach, seemed to recognize and stand for, the insurmountable number of nouns and adjectives and adverbs that had, in the past, confronted me on cold clean nights, thrilled with imagination. Like it was the final gathering of the stock market. Or like reggae music. Upbeat, strong and vibrant.

I stuck my key into the door only to find out that it was not locked. I took it to mean that Margarita was still inside in one of her more activated states. I gingerly walked through the dining room on my path to her study. I reclined on the love seat and looked at the squirrels. There were two of them, outside on the window seal scratching at the leaves as if they were trying to make them into something. They seemed to entertain me for a brief period. I moved from my position and sat at the desk.

I settled into the bland sun scorched darkness of the room like a bat in a Texas cave. Not upside sown, hanging from the fixtures, but adjusting myself in the chair, tossing and turning like some 45 rpm from the fifties. Little Richard like.

With the assistance of an artificial plant and its motley assemblage of wood chips at the bottom and a

set of mahogany framed prints of antiquated 18th century warships, I held my thoughts to Margarita and
what she would have to say concerning my sudden
change of plans.

I turned my head again. The woman who I had
just passed down the hall was standing right behind
me. I could feel her eyes against my skin. It felt like
she was trying to burn a hole through my structure.
"Where did you go?" She asked, not letting her hand
slip from under that cat.

Ever since the burial, she's developed a kind and
formal relationship with the neighbor's black Persian
cat. Formal to the extent that she allows it into the
house and regularly engages in monologue with it. I
do not particularly care for cats, but I could sympathize
with some cats. The big, predacious cats, panthers and
black cat. Black cats most of, just because I feel that
they get a bum rap. Like black cats, like black men. I
will probably have to take the rap when I foggle my
way on out of this relationship.

"I went for a little walk. I played in somebody's
pile of leaves a few blocks down."

"Well", she said, rubbing that organism on the
top of its head. "Things are not the way they used to
be, you've changed. You're just not the same person I
met four years ago. I don't know what happened. I
don't". She held her head down and walked over to
the window. My eyes caught that same little collection
of leaves on the ledge. She did not say anything. She
just looked right on out of that window, like she was
expecting it to write the answer on the board for her.
That abrupt Frenchness in her voice made me think of
the night I had first heard her speak. I wanted her
from that very instance. I still want her. But I also
want something that she will never be able to give me.
The whole scat was like a giant water beetle, a dichotomy. Here I am, not at all caring for her, or displaying
the same desire and admiration for her as I did for
writing. I craved my pen and adventure more than
her. The more I sat and watched her spit her silence

through the room, the more rapidly my mind begged to wander. I looked at her, altering my visual path to form a direct and straight line with the stormy grey eyes of the cat.

And after a few moments, her actions did not prove as bland or as irritating as her words had so many nights before the accident.

It was definite something odd about that cat and its eyes. Before I knew it, they had become cameras, television cameras. Entertainment tonight television cameras. This blond dame was perched up to a splendid row of date nut palms, the creamy blue winds and waves were behind her making her appear to look more appealing than she really was. I could see make up lines as thick as hash marks on her neck as I watched her point to wherever it was I was supposed to go. She kept pointing, telling me where to stand and shit like that. I felt like telling her to suck my you know what, but I did not for the sake of commercialism. She smiled a lot, especially when she was looking into the camera.

She started the interview by looking hardenly amber into the camera, with a microphone in her hand the size of my stick. She said, "Ladies and gentlemen, tonight's special guest on Entertainment Tonight, the multi-talented, author, screen-writer Barnett Love. Now Barnett, tell us, we know that the life of a play-write or screen writer is very different and extremely difficult to achieve. Tell us about your overnight success story."

"Well, Dianah, it all started with my last acquaintance, Lena Horne, We had been seeing an awful lot of each other, so much that I barely had time to write. And you know that I had been doing free-lance for most of my life. So really it was Lena's ideal. She said that she was willing to be the executive producer for anything that I put out, in the form of a screen play that is. And she meant it."

"Now, isn't it strange, and very risky for an individual to support a new and relatively unknown writer on their first major score?"

"Well Dianah, in the white community, maybe. There are so many repeat theme movies on the market, and more are coming out and being produced every year. That indicates that the market lacks creativity. I think that any cat that wants to write, and wants to write not to make a living, but rather to let the world in on his side of the picture, is not a risk. Firstly, ain't hardly no niggers gettin' money for their flicks and secondly, any story that a nigger will tell will be funny, sad, happy, metaphysical and different."

"I see Barnett. I wish you the best of luck on your new movie, "HOUSE OF SLAVES".

"Thank you, Dianah."

I was a success, I was a success, I was a success....Margarita had moved from the window. She was standing in front of the file cabinet. I selected to look at her for a moment. My bomber was hanging on the opened file cabinet. Just below it was a pair of my shoes. Inside of them, silvery, spring shoe horns with burgundy plastic heads. The springs arched themselves into the atmosphere as if they were twin bridges, linking two far and respected places. The pair was close enough together, and far away apart to give the impression of walking.

"You have a serious problem" she said in a melodramatic pitch.

"Me!"

"Yes, you. A problem. See, first of all, you do not pay attention. And if you do, it is extremely selective. You used to listen to me."

"I still listen to you. I just can't afford to pay attention any more. It seems that on the inside of me, that, that, I am only able to tune in to events. All of the dialogue is contrived inside of me the way I want it to be. I wanted very much to be the father of your child. I wanted very much to be the friend that took care of you when you were sick."

"Those are not bad suggestions, you know. Oui ?"

"I know, but they seem bad to me, on the inside, when they make me ignore the true desire of my flesh and spirit, writing. I don't know what it is. I tried so hard to get into you as I got into my writing. But,...I failed. And I'm not used to failing in anything. Maybe that was the only excuse that I could come up with, but it is the truth. I never wanted to hurt you, but I never wanted to hurt or deprive myself either."

She walked around some more. Back to the window, then over in front of me, taking a seat on her desk.

Softly she whispered in a penurious tone. "See that's what I mean. I'm only telling you this as a friend. We can work all of the details out in the future. But how can things get any better if you only think and talk of yourself? I have already lost my baby, I can't lose you too."

"I try to talk about others, but to be truthful, very few interest me. I try not to talk about Fontain and Tony and Willie Mitch and them, just 'cause I know that it will make me think of me, and of what I really want. Margarita, you must be able to discern, through all of this cloudiness, that I want to be with you. I do, I really do. I try to talk about others and think about others, but very few impress me to the extent of residual conservation."

She removed herself from the desk and jerked her head in disapproval. She had never been the type to cry. I guess it was that Surinam in her. Not even that night old what's his name was punching up on her. She didn't display a tear that night. A few high pitches whimpers, but no tears. Her eyes got glossy and her words, corrosive. "See, I told you that you had a problem."

I began to get on the defensive. I did not know why all of the pressure was needed. "And so do all of the other creatures and denizens of the universe. And right now, mine just happens to begin with the letter M."

"You will think about this with a level head one day. Might even end up in some mental Hospital. I just hope that you have insurance. You walking that tight rope right now and you ain't on the side of brilliance. You just a lazy nobody and that is all that you will ever be. I'm glad that Naja is not around to see how much she lacked a father. Or better yet, what I called a father, and once.....a man."

This was the last time that I graced myself in her house. I started singing to myself. Just to let her know that I was about to go into the insane asylum.

> "I want to make you understand,
> that I'm talking
> about an all life plan.
> Dancing across the room,
> ending all too soon.
> Hurry don't be late,
> I can hardly wait,
> I say to myself when...."

"Hurry don't be late", I said to myself. Margarita had ventured off into the den. I heard the music come on. Sade. She was probably the only thing left that we both enjoyed with mutual admiration. Next to Naja that is. But she was gone. Gone in the spirit but not from my heart, or my eyes, or my tears. The music took my visions away slowly.

> "Grandma came to see
> something she could not believe
> how could her girl be
> so naive.
> tar baby, tar baby
> told the secret she concealed.
> that big old smile of yours
> could turn the wind into a song.
> how could I have doubted
> honey it's with me that you belong

115

tar baby, tar baby
I love you so.
like a brand new blade
you cut into my life
cut through, decades
like a hot coal on ice..."

I left that modest dwelling with just enough money for the bus. I wanted to call someone, but Tiana was out of the question. It hurt me a little to accept that the forces of life had not manifested the way it was on TV, for me and Margarita.

It was like left and right for the rest of the day. I personally preferred this way and that away. But sometimes, it was a lot simpler to explain things in terms of left and right. I see why historians and politicians and journalist always refer to things with the prefixes right and left. People are more concerned it seems, with labeling shit with labels and shit, that they hardly ever consider the relatively, or the expansive nature of time. That it is always the same, in limbo, through death, beyond life, with women.

Funny, how a mother fucker can get lost into himself, like he has no problems, no worries. But that is what expression is all about. Distorting the individual precepts of time, space, and gravity. Sometimes I think so much and so hard that it feels like I am above myself, as if I can do anything in the world. And I know that I can do anything in the world, and I will.

Two hours and four buses had past. I was about twenty two miles from Margarita and approximately one half of a block from that white-wall dwelling of a cave that I used to consider home. Two towering oaks and a middle-age popular tree greeted me with a windily welcome of multi-hued leaves. It made me feel like a little boy on his first day walking home from school by himself. Tiana had said that Tony had been staying there. I was past a large fence of sticker bushes when I saw a big colorless truck. Had big huge wheels and was real muddy. The rest of the extended environment

116

was still the same. I rang the doorbell. Somebody was there, I heard voices outside of the door.

"See man, that ain't shit that's why we behind now."

"What you talking about? Don't dog me, I'm down with South Africa, but my heart is buried in this problem over here. Fuck that concern myself with South Africa shit. I think it is just another attempt to stick a pacifier in niggers mouths and frankly I take it as an insult."

I rang the doorbell again. This time I was greeted with a cigarette smoked, "It's open, com' on in."

The knob was turned with a mild bit of hesitation on my behalf. With the door partially opened, I could see in the deepness of the carpet, that several parties had occurred, or either that someone had changed the oil of some motor vehicle in the living room. The same blue, Rubbermaid garbage container was still standing guard at the door. Chairs rumbled and Leon first approached. His face shined with a beer smile. "Gash, thought that you were dead. Psych. Naw, heard you been on that vagabond tip."

"I nodded my head in agreement. Tony stood up next. He was sitting in front of my old apple. Looked like he had added a hard disk to it.

"Well, if it ain't the one and only sleaze bum supreme. Don't call a mother fucker 'ey?"

"It's good to be back". I stretched out my hand for five and he pushed it out of the way.

"Don't give me that shake your hand bull shit. You better hug me mother fucker."

I grabbed him like a long lost brother, and the same was complementary of Leon.

"Wish that I could chat a little bit longer, but I got Geronimo on my dick on your machine." Tony abruptly stated, making quick strides back to his seat.

Leon folded his arms and sighed a deep breath. "He been hooked on that game ever since he got it."

"What is it?" I asked , wanting at the same time to play it myself.

117

"The Ancient Art of War. It's pretty stimulating. He thinks that by practice tactic of war against the computer that it will get him ready for the impending revolution."

"Man, fuck you!" Tony exclaimed, not turning to follow his remark.

"Fuck for ya mother fucker."

"Is this what has been up since I've been gone?" I questioned. It was like I was expecting them to have bounded volumes of fables for me, documenting all of the shit I'd missed while I was out on my quest for the holy Grail.

He took his time again and released another deep sigh. he seemed to have become somewhat more patient over the past years, and on the opposite side, it appeared that Tony had gotten more creative. He gave me a copy of the SUMMARY OF NATIONAL SECURITY STUDY MEMORANDUM 200: IMPLICATIONS OF WORLD WIDE POPULATION GROWTH FOR U.S. SECURITY AND OVERSEAS INTEREST. It was a 250 page document that was dated December 10, 1974. He said that it explains how Brent Scowcroft. Henry Kissinger, George Bush and then chief of Staff Dick Cheney sterilized more than 10 million women in Brazil. Ninety-five percent of which were of African descent. I told him that I would read it and asked about Fontain and Monroe, about the babes they were seeing and the new party spots. He told me that of all people, Willie was getting married. When I asked him about the business, he told me that he'd consider it. But right now, he was in the process of re-evaluating his life space.

"You know", he said. "I've had to cool down. A nigger can't sling it like he used to."

"I know what you mean." Tony commented. "Nigger got to have them "contra-aids: to keep a niggers dick from rotting off."

"You been smelling too much paint." I darted. Marvin Gaye was filtering through the air rather efficiently. Sounding just right from any position my

118

body occupied. Then I began to think about it all. A bad habit of mine I guess. About the music. About hypothetical constructs. About Margarita. About Naja and about words. Tony looked like he was taking a break from the monochrome display of the monitor. He rubbed the undergrowth of hair sewn in his chin and wedged a cigarette in between the auspices of his lips. He looked over at us, then down, feeling around the outside of his pockets, shifting the square around from corner to corner. He pulled the chair back from the table, stood oak tall aside the table and felt the region of his pockets again.

"You got a light." He asked, letting the smoke dangle from his lips the same way a spider's web drifts in the wind when partially obstructed from its foundation.

Tony threw him a small lighter. He caught it with one hand. The flame flared as high as his nose. "Can I at least get a lighter that won't burn my nose off?

"If you would move your hands and fingers then maybe you will be alright."

"Gash., who asked your monkey ass to come back?

"Nobody. Nothing like a change of scenery to stimulate a wondering mind."

"So when you gonna tell us about your travels?" Tony questioned, with his square finally in smoking warp.

"As soon as you get off of my computer, the sooner you can read it. If I'm gonna waste thought on you, I might as well have it stored so I can waste it on other people too."

CHAPTER 12
PUBLICATION

It was a huge adjustment. Not having anyone to call, to eat with, to sit across the table from, to gaze into their deep emerald black eyes, and melt with the faint whisper of my words, or lyrics as they would seem to she. She.

I was at this bar. Do not worry or concern yourself with the name, you never heard of it. Anyway, I was at this bar. Saloon, Eatery. Whatever. I guess that so far, if you have learned anything about me at all, that you can tell that I live, or spend and endure, most of my pestilence in a sometimes, seems to be, appears to be, type of sort of atmosphere. But see, to me that is what it is all about, the unknown. The unknown is what we are all looking for -- answers.

There was supposed to be this band. I think jazz. "I live in midtown." The dame next to me, replied in response to her associate opposite the table. Then it happened. Let me start from the very beginning, which happens to start in the middle of a quick stare at the woman next to me. Her man was definitely a wimp. Every time he ordered a brew, it would be the kind that would exceed the three dollar mark and require the "anticipatory appeasement" of a wedge of lime.

And of his date, she was sweating him.

After a while, the couple began to bore me. I eyed their waitress, my waitress, to come over and take care of me. I happened to be writing at the time.

Her hair was the color of a tomato near the end of the summer, her legs thick and her ass was not the most convex seating arrangement and her eyes sparkled with a champagne grey.

"What are you doing?" She asked, permitting her torso to bend just enough to let me steal a peak of her tightly firm pectorals.

121

"Writing," I returned, lifting my pen from the page. "Rolling Rock please."

"What are you writing about." She arched her back, bringing to the fore of that cotton blouse, her nipples and breast. Filling my vision like a pair of hand-squeezed balloons. From the back that is.

"About a relic of the past that never existed. I just have a writing problem. Especially when it takes my drinks too long to reach my stomach."

"I mean. What are you working on now?"

"A buzz hopefully."

"O.K., if I hurry back, will you talk to me?" With hands firmly on her hips and the hemline of that tight knit skirt showing the outlined, delicate, meticulous highlights of her appendages, ebbing just enough to let me know I wanted to pin her to the mat. I nodded in agreement, following her ass around the room as phenomenon benefundatum.

She came back. Immediately, tensing a pose that made my eyes, along with other parts of my anatomy, recognize that there truly existed a overman.

"She looked me in the eye", as Tom Petty would sing. Then we started to talk. Of painted moons, and things of that nature. I told her that I was a writer. She shunned the ideal innately. Then excepting it more and more with the rising tide of my words. "So what do you write, in specific?" She questioned plainly.

"Whatever is to be written, documented in word, on paper, on disk, in the mind of others; beyond the voice even. Even the things communication will never explain."

"Do you write about yourself."

I paused. The band was about to perform. The drummer was beating his sticks around the blackened auricle above the stage as if he was a boy with two pockets full of marbles.

"I write of what I know. The way I see shit. Like I'm god by nature and so is everybody else."

She looked into my eyes as if she was trying to break me down, intimidate me. She had informed me

122

that she was an actress and that she knew someone in publishing. I pressed on, leading the conversation like a grand master of chess.

Like most women, she was all about money. That's why I liked women, the got good heads on their shoulders. Fontain has broken it down to the fact that bros like us are supposed to mack hoes to make them maximize productivity. He says otherwise, civilization would lose out to soap operas and malls. She tried to check me too.

"Why do you drink that cheap fisherman beer. That's the cheapest beer in the nation."

"What's it to you."

"Style, it's about style, flare, glamour. That's what it takes if you want to be an actress."

"Like yourself I suppose?"

"Yes, style. Wouldn't you agree?"

The first set had started somewhere around 10:02 p.m., plus or minus a few minutes. The bass player followed after the percussionist lead with a lascivious, heart-pounding, thumb-bruising solo. I answered her question, I think. "But as for style, 'ay, I have never considered it to be of elite nobility. I never could understand why a person would buy a particular kind of brew, for five dollars, for six dollars a six. Especially when it is more suitable economically that is, to purchase the same material product, with less stamps on the bottle, for a lower price."

I found myself trying real hard not to use the universal, genderless synonym for a person in her presence -- nigger. I slipped a few times but It wasn't really that big of a deal.

"You're cheap," she opened in a firm voice. "What do you like to do?"

"Like to eat. Like to sleep. Like to dance. Like to fuck."

She tilted her shoulders back, clearing her throat but not really coughing. "You've broken my train of thought, but only for the moment."

For the first time, I noticed that she began to twinkle at the eyes. Maybe an hallucinatory perception on my behalf, or maybe Orca coming to the surface for air. But I'm more than certain that that sudden swing to blues by the band, contributed the "mostest" to the milieu.

She left and I returned to dwelling. The saxophone player asked if anyone wanted to sing. What the hec'.

My body took over the beat instantly, like it would the flu. The crowd, ritzy and supportive. I see why musicians and singers tend to undergo mental transformations undertaking such a profession. It's addictive but not overpowering enough to make me swindle my nose down to a Caucasian slice. But never the less, as so many times previous, I was live at my best, if ever such a construct there was. Like being and nothingness, nothingness brought into being and being as nothing all rolled up into one steel-belted radial. Special, I tell ya.

What made it so good was that I made up my own words.

"I know everywhere I've been.
I know everywhere I've been.
I know my life is ful' of sin."

I saw what I wanted to be.
I saw what I wanted to be.
I saw you sleeping with me."

That line drove them rabid

"You' skin so soft, I won't slo' down.
Yo' skin so soft, I won't slow down.
Jus' let me darling, jus' let me play around."

"Baby, baby, baby,
Baby, baby, baby,

124

baby, baby, baby, baby, baby, baby."

I returned to my cheap ass fishermen brew. They applauded, completely out of sympathy. It took me awhile to reflect on what had just occurred. Was it important, significant? I had dreamed of singing in front of a live audience at least a billion times, each through a different method of analysis. Some were so enjoyable that if I thought about them for too long, a smile would stretch across my face.

Music, I tell ya', it's beyond Big Mac's and Krystal burgers. Even above the explanation of a collective oligarchy -- which is real to me.

The waitress came back over to the table. I had learned now that her name was Nina and that she did not appreciate or respect any of the Russian literary artist of the late nineteenth century. We left the joint together, she got off earlier than usual she said. My truck was parked out back.

She took me to this little, large and quaint Chinesc or Japanese or Korean of Thai restaurant. I had always wanted to know why people ate with sticks when forks or hand were more accessible, especially white people. I guess that she thought that it was cool, retro-chic, eating with sticks. Give me a fork any day, this is America.

She offered to buy me dinner. I refused. I explained to her in about two paragraphs how it was not the move trying to get full on rice. As we waited, I began to play special attention to her paleness. It made my flesh crawl for a while but not enough to alter my course of horniness. I did except a beer however. I waited some more.

"So where are you from originally?" I questioned, not like it made a difference.

She flung her hair the way white folks so often did and supported her chin on the palm of her right hand. "We already discussed that. I can tell what you are thinking about."

"What?" I questioned. Again she gazed deeply into my eyes. The way she did at the cafe when she first began to ask me questions. As if she was holding her breath under water, holding it until she reached the top of the surface, she finally returned. "Fucking".

There was no need to hesitate.

"Have you ever considered changing your name to sister Ruby or something like that?"

She acted as if she had blown off my remarks completely, going on to her directed train of thought. "I like to fuck but a girl got to watch out for shit like Advanced Immune Deficiency Syndrome. Aren't you afraid of AIDS?"

"Yea, I'm afraid of anything that is third generation but that's why I carry litmus paper around. Every man would want to. Sick a couple of strips in the old wishing well and presto, color change or not. Fail safe."

They brought over the beer. Two cans of Bush. They even brought matching glasses. I persuaded her to turn them over as a political statement. Personally I preferred the can.

The waiter returned a few seconds later. Shrimp fried rice and two egg rolls. She requested of him to prepare it to go. Like a crane she was, when she stood up. She walked in a manner that made her legs do all of her communicating. By looking at them one would find it rather surprising and advanced that she could talk.

With bill in hand, she dug insensitively into a little black bucket of a pocket book, pulling out what appeared to be an eyeglass case. She wore glasses. I had never imagined that a Nina would wear glasses.

Outside, the gleaming dominion of buildings deterrently inhibited my eyes from wanting to see more. I saw the streets but was not with them. I heard the music but was not in tune. I branched out into a desperate and narrow train of thought, as if my eyes were closed but they were open, on the inside that is.

Like looking up into the sun with them closed. And she continued to talk.

"You know, my father would kill me if he knew that I was with a black man." She threw out, making it sound like some amusement park.

I did want to come back at her quickly, so I thought and paid strict intentness to the way in which I constructed my sentences.

"Why don't we stop and call him." Her smile widened with each word.

"You are funny. Your just as funny now as you were when you told me that you were a writer. I could see through you all along."

"I am a writer." It was all too complicated. Nina had known me only for a few hours, yet she believed that she had the ability to see through me."

"If you were a real writer you would have a book out on the market. Then at least some one that did not know of you, in some far and distant portion of the world would learn of you. If you were a real writer you would not just settle for writing for pleasure, you would turn that pleasure over into fortune. Can we agree that we can have fame without fortune?"

"That is possible," I replied. "How much further do we have to go?"

"Just four more lights and a left turn."

Her apartment, flat grey with carpet and mineral blue with glass. The TV set was on. I was still thinking about Nina's comments from the auto. She shared this place with her brother. They both were originally born in Norfolk.

"Make yourself at home. No one will be by here tonight. I'm in the kitchen."

A red a gold poster advertising a past tour of the Moscow Ballet hovered above the fire place with amplified balance. Below it were pictures of her family and several crystal ducks.

Passing by his bedroom, I observed what had to be seven or eight computers. On desk tops, file cabinets and milk crates their omnipotence towered higher than any mountain. Atari computers, 800 series, I think. Four of which with color monitors. I figured that they all had to be turned on at the same time, synchronized in one base circuit. All were alternating in hues on every ten second interval. The color was like an attitude, fierce, shorn and undisposed. So undisposed that I began to stare into the mendicant demureness of one. Just like a dream it was, with the exception of color no doubt.

My dream had something to do with being in court. There was only one chair and I occupied it. To my immediate right were twelve, hand-constructed an simple designed computer cubicles. You know, the kind that allow for maximizing space, perfect posture and plastic screw covers. And on each was one IBM desk top. As unworthy as they appeared, I stared them directly in their output devices -- I was not close enough to observe any serial ports settings and therefore unable to discern their actual sex.

I tried to lift myself up and approach them, but both my wrist and feet were shackled securely to the chair. They were not as tight as they were that night with Robert. The stormy grey judges panel opened in an elevator type fashion. Behind it appeared an extraordinary sized cathode ray tube. A single red plasma arrow doubly served as both prompt and cursor -- Maybe because they are the same thing. Above it was what I suspected to be an automatic speech synthesizer. I was correct. With the prompt came words, with the words, came sound.

"What do you have to say for yourself?" It said in an electronically sexy way.

"What should I say?" I asked, honestly trying to figure out what was going on.

"How do you plead to the charges against you?"

"What charges?"

"Being dedicated and loyal to the powers divine in all of nature, being dedicated to being your own person, being unwilling to pursue avenues of greed and lastly, being the murderer of two printer, two monitors and one modem. How do you plead?"

Although I did not consider myself to display a penchant for law and order, I did respect myself. I opened. "Your machine languageness, I must admit, I do not even think that death, I mean a blown circuit board would prevent me from learning more about myself. And as for law, no man-made law runs paramount to the verdant complexities of nature. So I guess I must concur with the charges."

She blinked on for a while. Evidently linking up with the monitors of the jury. She blinked. I waited.

Then finally, the prompt read, "you are sentenced to take a urine test."

I moved about in rejection. Taking the wood off of the chair with the hand cuffs, shaking my head, thrashing in vain. I commented. "There is no such concept as freedom. Where's my freedom? I tell you, I don't have it if I have to ask, do I?"

Snapping out of it, I realized that only the monitors had been blinking. There were no plasma prompts, IBM displays or huge cathode ray tube. Just orange and green, rust and jade and peach and blue.

I wondered how long had I been dreaming. Not too long I suppose. A couple of minutes, just enough for some impromptu make-believe.

I could hear food frying in the kitchen and could smell bacon in the air. I thought about my life, about my writing, about education, about the realness of human life, being and about what Nina had spoken of earlier in the car. I had pontificated on shit like this before, and would probably do so again in the future, just probably in a different combination. Then I thought of Kant and scuttled into the kitchen.

"...The
peculiarity of a
truly human life
lies in the fact
that man has to

create himself
by his own vol-
untary efforts."

I was not amazed to see her eating and cooking at the same time.

"I'm making you a few BLT's if you don't mind." She said as she turned the eye of her gas stove down.

Within a few minutes, both sandwiches were past tense, playing merrily with my gastric juices. She suggested that we go move to her room and listen to some music. Again, I could not resist the temptation of gawking at one of the numerous computer monitors perched in her brother's room.

You can tell drastically, the difference between a flat kept by a woman in gross comparison to her beastly counterpart. And not just because of the neatly random scattering of piles of Elle, Taxi, and Vogue magazines either. We talked more.

"So what have you been up to beside acting and working?" I asked. I did not really care for the conversation but I did want to, somehow, get her back on the subject that we entertained shortly in the truck.

She responded with a simple "oh".

"Alphabets 'ey. Now we don't want to break that train of thought, now do we?"

She returned with a coy smile and a finger sign.

"You probably do more things with that finger than you will ever let me do." I stated firmly, just knowing that soon, I would be pinning her to the mat. She kept looking down, in the region of my crotch. I acted as if I did not notice

"I wonder sometimes, what it would be like to be black", she stated.

"I can dig it. I wonder what it would be like to be white, and have no rhythm."

From the way that she revealed herself when stretching, I noticed that she curved like the letter W. "Wow" accentuated her subtle construction, if any, a single, lonely, modicum of a conglomeration of Arabic letters ever could. Repeat after me; wow... And that short, sashed peeling of an outfit, did much more to attract, and retain my lewdness as did the manner in which the locks of her rosy red hair, selfishly contained her completed fortune. And of her lips; lasciviously thin luxuriously, finicky, candy, like an Autumn fire of sticks and rusty hued leaves, burning until total exhaustion.

"What did you mean when you said that I was not a real writer?"

"Real writers:, she said. "Are about something. They are about more than living adventurous lives and putting it all down in ink. They are about letting the world in on their personal secret. They are brave, fearless and dedicated to nothing but vision. It's a matter of attention. Attention. Let people know that you are out there. When you do this, well, call it what you want but you will feel better, knowing that your works are out on the market for people to love or avoid."

I had no further questions. I stood away from her and started opening the buttons to my pants. She looked at me like she was waiting on the Heinz ketchup to come out. I only needed a few seconds. I went back towards her and towered above her with my placid member looking her in the face. The temperature change was all I needed to bring about stiffness.

"It's wonderful." She said. "It's sex, it even smells of sex. She took it out of her mouth for a moment, rubbing it all over her face, kissing it, keeping her eyes shut, placing it against the side of her cheek. She seemed happy to see that it was a tad bit longer than her head.

Lying her on her back, I pulled her shirt over her head and raised that sashed skirt waist height. I was playing with her now. I wanted to go for the old in/ out right then, but I did not. Instead I grabbed her panties with one hand and slid the deep in between the gullies of her organ. I saw them become drenched with her own liquids and almost disappear completely inside of her pert mound of pubic hair. She wiggled timorously, not even once taking her hand from my dick. Pulling at each opportunity to place me inside of her. Finally, I pulled the dampened material from between her wetness and held them to the side, ripping them somewhat, accidently falling into her heat. She tried to prevent me from exploring the unctuous blackness of her soma by wrapping her legs inside of mine. No contest.

"Is that it?" I asked. " The way you want it?"

Clenching the cover and biting on her bottom lip were the only replies I could understand. Everything else were nettled, high-pitched sounds. I continued. I thrashed the structure of my body like it was comprised of fine and slender metal extensions. Throwing her into the air, on to the bed, with jerky, forceful motions. As if in a drunken stupor; dragging her, burning her bottom over the sheets, extending her off of the bed, on to the floor with prompt aggression. Positioning her mostly with her parted legs and feet. Entering and pounding and clutching and sweating like primates in the rain forest.

I wanted ever so much to pull her by her hair; not in an effort to hurt her, just trying to hold her around me a little longer, a little tighter, a lot wetter, it was, then. Our sweat continued to evince its force. Sinking profoundly into the pink cotton, transforming it instantly into burgundy. She held steady, beneath me like France under Bonaparte.

The lights were on, that made it better, or at least, it was perceived as better. I had always hated going to parties and night clubs for the same reason. But also because of the price and due to the fact that I could not peep all the hoes. I felt great.

Three sets of five had past. Now, I was no longer thinking of the individual. I could not even dwell on the statement she made concerning how she knew "it would be like this" or that her "daddy would kill her if he knew". It was not as important as relegating all activity in memorial of Margarita.

132

The more reality suggested to me that it was not her, the harder I tried to teleport her structure and imagery under me; the more I realized that it was not her, that it was white, that it was bland and preferred NutraSweet.

I continued to drill her, to put my meat plunging through her back.

I left her there, thanked her for the meal and broke. It was a little after two and with one nutt released, I still had plenty of time to make it to Willie's bachelor party.

I had just enough coins to make it to the other side of town. Stopping to get some gas, I bought a newspaper. Some flashy derelict passed by me in a 289 Mustang hardtop, windows down with Jon Astley's - *Jane's Getting Serious.* I moved my head up and down in a eagerly jerky motion for nearly ten yards, glanced over the paper and divided my attention evenly between it and my five block journey. Two blocks from my destination, at an intersection imposed with plenty of instructional icons and looping electric cables, music from another car entered my haven of invulnerable destination. The car indiscernible, the song *Save A Prayer* by Duran Duran. I stayed with me for about nine or ten yards of side walk.

I first saw that charming stone of a house from across the street. Angling towards it like a hit man, with jacket expiring intentions that only a man with a gun afraid of cars would have when crossing the street; avoiding all bright lights and metallic objects, not on purpose, but by choice. I was still singing *Save A Prayer* to myself, substituting the lines that I did not recall with an isolated whistle or two.

First, there were the stairs. Fabricated to attain that needed umph, the insolent traveler so frequently sighs. Four of them, followed by six, followed by four. Each at angles of ninety degrees of one another.

Loud and dubious vulgarities and the sort were heard even before I began my ascension.

"That's why I became a lawyer. I'm down to protect the criminals, I'm down to send the police to jail. Anybody with a little sense can see that all it is about from the home side is tag the brilliant mother fucker before he penetrates the mind of someone else."

Black Magic was into his law.

"You don't give a real fuck." Willie returned.

"What you got to say about it? You 'bout to marry Thelma Lou up in hear. That alone proves your senility. He quickly returned.

I stopped looking at that abominable deformity of a Magnolia and went for the screen door.

Willie by the time I entered had responded. "Why you wanna play me like Any Griffin?"

The laughing continued even after the slamming of the screen door.

"Leon came from out of the back room. He looked at me and concocted a barren reproduction of a smile.

"Gash., welcome. I got the gun powder in the back."

Another conversation had erupted behind us. Fontain held an astute dialogue with a gallon of Crown Royal while Willie and Tony and Black divided their discussion between free enterprise and perceived plots of extermination.

"I'm glad to see that you are doing well for yourself." I opened, grabbing the papers and tray.

"I will excel in whatever I do you know I'm God by nature." He said with a defamatory loftiness, turning to take on the plush encampment of stairs to his left.

"I followed him and returned," so you a Hyundai now, 'ay?"

"We've gotten rather sophisticated, wouldn't you say?" Like a gentleman and scholar, he afforded me the privilege of test rat and allowed me into the room before him. He switched on the lights and reclined in a wooden rocking chair. There was a red velvet pillow on the seat, added, I suppose, for comfort.

134

I nodded my head in agreement but replied, "Pope would argue for arrogance."

"Still got to be iconoclastic, would you not say?" He rolled his eyes. Leon always rolled his eyes when we challenged one another on issues of survival.

"A nigger got to question everything." I added.

"Everything", he agreed." Bus' up one of them incense."

"This ain't my camp."

"Not the point mother fucker, don't have to be."

"Aw fuck you, you new Coke drinking scab."

"It's better than digging buggers," He threw out. I passed him the joint. We continued.

"You got to do us a favor." He stated.

"What?"

"You got to promise never to let our school of thought fade from the annals of existence. And Gash, you the only one who can do it G. You got to care enough about our collective interaction to teach others, or at least let them in on the fun. See, we all from an area, and people, who blend with the world through the family. Other mother fuckers ain't had that. That's some heavy shit. Heavy."

I thought about what he was saying, it was some weighted shit alright. All of our lives, we had been taught to achieve, achievement was all that we knew. Pulling out a tiny package of sniff-sniff. He hit a one on one and continued.

"And nowadays, if a nigger get erratic off that white, it's all over. It's some niggers I would give my last dime to, in here, tonight. We use to think that you were crazy back in the day. You talked about starting a school and writing and nothing else.

Leon then stood, stretching his appendages until extension was complete. I remained and wrote.

On the wall was a head and tail poster. Pink and green and front and back string bikinis no doubt. The pinkness of the room and its hardwood floor did more for my pen than my personal constructs. And that 2 BLACK 2 STRONG didn't hurt the ambience ei-

135

ther. I will probably never contemplate again, the visual details, the physical aberrations and the continuous consternation that put me under at the time. Death, no. But the satisfaction of living in a world of illusion, yes.

Of Margarita I thought. I did love, her, but in the same exact breath, I could not and did not perceive that such a transition was possible. One of many she was, attempting to examine the realm of space where the pen drains of ink and the cartridge completes itself of ribbon, never to write or control the destination of another word of phrase of sentence or question again. Cluttering her brain with the vilest of concepts. Like assorted pencils in a retired desk drawer. Or like the feeling a person gets when they only get fifteen joints out of a quarter bag.

I went back into the living room. Surprisingly, this was the first time in nearly two hours and six pages of a memo pad. There was a bag of chips on the table. I grabbed them. They were empty. Still music.

> "Keep away girl,
> this one's all mine.
> Keep away girl,
> this one's all mine."

I wedged myself into the kitchen, into another conversation.

"So man, when you want to do that?" Willie asked, holding his belly at me as if it was some new weapon.

"Do what?"

"Publication."

"I'm down now. What you got?"

"Well, I just got a hook-up with this publishing house. In fact its mine. What you got for me?"

"You won't Jew me out the money will ya?" I paused. "Novels, Plays, Short stories. They straight, I like them."

"I know, I believe in you."

"Self-determination is some strong stuff."

"Brilliance can't be avoided, just launched from one population to another."

"I can do anything."

"Undoubting", he added, folding his arms and supporting himself against the counter. "I already got a three city marketing plan made out for 10,000 copies."

"Good, saves me some work."

"I never doubted myself, just the opinions of others. If a nigger want anything, got to do it they self. He tapped me on the back and said, "We gone do it, all of us. Master Sam gone have to kill us to stop us and Africa knows he trying his best to exterminate us. Especially people like you G."

I turned away a remodeled person. Freedom or grace, what's the difference? One never was and the other, self-determined; like scholarship, like pride, like friends, like sex.

I tried to take myself to an even deeper level by looking at the phone cable and next, at the green and grey and pink and rose and white stripped mattress and box-springs. I lost.

Again, I turned to memories of Margarita. Maybe it was the music, maybe it was me. I wanted her, forever, like wanting it to be fall forever and ever and ever, Amenophis. It had to be the flesh, mostly. The simple and compact ideal of penetrating such a magnificent composition of appearance and structure. There was no love. There would never be.

Leon had told me before, that I was an eccentric. That I was the only one able to drive a car around with an entire Shark's jaw on the rear view mirror and get away with it. He said it was a gift.

ABOUT THE AUTHOR

Torrance Stephens is originally from Memphis, Tennessee. He attended Morehouse College where he studied, psychology, biology and chemistry. He received a master's degree in Educational Psychology and Measurement from Atlanta University and a Ph.D. in Counseling from Clark Atlanta University. He has lived in Nigeria, Senegal, South Africa and several other African countries working with Africare International and conducting Infectious disease research. He is the author of several books including a novel, poems, essays and several collections of short prose. He was an Assistant Professor at Emory University in the Rollins School of Public Health in Atlanta for more than 14 years and until recently, as Associate Professor and Health Education/Health Promotion Track Coordinator for the MPH program at Morehouse School of Medicine in the Department of Community and Preventive Medicine. He is the father of two and currently lives in Palmetto, Georgia, and teaches Statistics at Clark Atlanta University in the Departments of Psychology and School of Education.

www.ingramcontent.com/pod-product-compliance
Lightning Source LLC
Chambersburg PA
CBHW060749180626
46818CB00002B/512